"You think I care about *that*!"

Sara demanded fiercely. "You think that *money* is more important to me than love?"

"I think it odd that such a scheming woman could be such a caring granddaughter," Luke answered coldly. "And I warn you," he said harshly. "No matter what your grandmother wants, no child of mine will ever be used as a hostage to fortune."

Pride made Sara stand there and face him. "I assure you that the last thing I want is to have your child, Luke," she said. "The assumption that we would have children was Gran's."

"No, I suppose you wouldn't want children, would you?" Suddenly he was so angry that she was mystified. His voice was bitter as he added, "Your sort never do."

FRANCES RODING is a new name in the Harlequin romance series. However, we feel sure that the writing style of this British-based author will soon make her popular with romance readers everywhere.

Books by Frances Roding

HARLEQUIN PRESENTS
1052—OPEN TO INFLUENCE

HARLEQUIN ROMANCE
2901—SOME SORT OF SPELL

FRANCES RODING

man of stone

Harlequin Books

TORONTO • NEW YORK • LONDON
AMSTERDAM • PARIS • SYDNEY • HAMBURG
STOCKHOLM • ATHENS • TOKYO • MILAN

Harlequin Presents first edition April 1989
ISBN 0-373-11163-0

Original hardcover edition published in 1988
by Mills & Boon Limited

CHAPTER ONE

'So THERE'S no money, then; no money, no house, no anything.'

Her stepsister's light voice had hardened fractionally, and Sara winced as she looked up and saw a matching hardening in Cressy's pale blue eyes.

This was so difficult for Cressy, she acknowledged painfully. She herself had been more prepared. Her father had warned her only a few months ago about the precariousness of his financial position.

Once a fashionable and sought-after painter, he had no illusions about himself or his talent. In the days when he had commanded large sums for his paintings, he had spent lavishly. Now those days were gone, and it seemed that even the Chelsea house had not actually been owned by him, but was on a lease from someone else.

With his death that lease was cancelled, which meant... Which meant that from the end of the month they would all three of them be homeless, Sara recognised bleakly.

For herself, she could perhaps have managed. Although she had always been the one to run the house, to do her father's books and take charge of the household, she had had a secretarial training that, with a little polishing, could equip her to earn her own living. But there were other things to be taken into consideration.

'So what are you going to do about Tom?' Cressy asked her in a hard voice. 'There's no way I can take charge of him, and he won't be able to stay on at school. There won't be any money for private school fees now.'

Tom, the eight-year-old half-brother born of the marriage between her father and Cressy's mother. Tom, with his delicate constitution and his tendency towards asthma attacks. Tom, who, she had known since they first gave her the news of the accident, would be her responsibility.

It was pointless wishing that Cressy was different; Cressy was Cressy.

She looked across the kitchen at her beautiful stepsister and sighed.

'I never understood why on earth my mother married your father,' Cressy complained. 'Mother was so beautiful. She could have married anyone.'

By anyone, Cressy meant a man with money, and Sara neglected to point out that when they had first married her father had been comparatively wealthy. Instead, she said softly, 'They were in love, Cressy.'

'Oh, love . . .' She tossed her head, making shimmering beams of light dance off the carefully lightened curls. 'Who cares about that? When I marry, it will be to a wealthy man. *You'll* have to take charge of Tom, of course.'

Sara didn't question her abruptness, nor the hard determination in her voice. She knew Cressy too well. Others were so easily deceived by Cressy's sugar-sweet façade, she thought sadly. They saw the blonde hair and the blue eyes, the fragile bone structure and the deliciously curved body, and they didn't look any further.

It wasn't that she was jealous. Well, at least, not totally, she admitted painfully, unable to deny that it would have been rather nice to look as femininely precious as Cressy. She felt that she was plain in comparison, five foot four, with hair the colour of polished hazelnuts when the sun shone on it, and at other times a rather dull brown. Likewise, her eyes reflected the chameleon quality of her personality, green one moment, hazel another.

She was a quiet, rather shy girl, used to effacing herself, used to standing in the shadow of her far more self-assured stepsister, even though Cressy was her junior by two years.

Cressy's father had been an actor, and Cressy was determined to follow in his footsteps. She had just left drama school, and had actually been cast in a very minor role in a West End play.

They had all gone to see it. Even Tom, who had been home from the private boarding-school he attended in Berkshire. Cressy had been very good. Her father had been very proud of her, Sara remembered with a faint tinge of loneliness.

There were times when she had thought that her father wished that Cressy had been his daughter, rather than herself. She took after her mother, apparently, but she had no real way of knowing if this was true, because Lucy Rodney had died when Sara was born.

She had got on well enough with Laura, Cressy's mother. She and her father had been a well-matched pair, both of them enjoying the luxurious and rather fast-paced life that James Rodney embraced.

That was one of the reasons that there was no money. Her father must have thought himself immortal, Sara thought wryly. He had certainly never thought to make any provision for a tragedy such as the one which had just overwhelmed them.

She had read about the avalanche that had buried an alpine village in her morning paper. It had been lunch time before she learned that her father and Laura had been killed in it.

Now there were just the three of them; an odd and very disparate family unit, consisting of two young women and one half-grown child. But Cressy was already making it plain that she was going to opt out of that unit, and so it would just be the two of them. Tom and herself.

Sara wanted to protest, to remind her stepsister that Tom was their shared responsibility, but she thought of Tom's strained, pale face, and the way he always shied away from the often acerbic Cressy and instead she said quietly, 'Perhaps that would be best.'

She had to turn away to avoid seeing the relieved satisfaction in Cressy's eyes.

'Well, it is the most sensible solution, darling. After all, looking after a small and rather sickly child is hardly my scene, is it? Besides, I may get a chance at a role in an American soap. I could hardly take Tom out to California with me. Not with his asthma.'

Sara forbore to comment that, on the contrary, the hot, dry climate would probably do their half-brother a world of good. She had far more weighty things on her mind than Cressy's selfishness. For one thing, where on earth were they going to live? Without the house, the small salary she could bring in was hardly going to provide comfortable accommodation for a young woman and an eight-year-old child.

'Darling, I must fly. I'm due out tonight...'

'Cressy, we still haven't discussed where we're going to live,' Sara protested. 'We lose this house at the end of the month.'

'Oh, haven't I told you? Jenneth has a spare room in her flat, which she offered me.' The blue eyes hardened. 'Look, Sara, be practical for once in your life. Why on earth don't you get in touch with your mother's family?'

'My mother's family?' Sara repeated stupidly. 'But...'

'Oh, come on, darling. Use your head. Your mother came from a wealthy Cheshire family. We all know that! All right, so they refused to have anything to do with her when she defied her parents and ran away to marry your father, but that's years ago now. If you turn up on their doorstep, destitute, with a small child in tow, they're bound to take you in.'

'Cressy!' Sara was horrified, and it showed. She was also bewildered. From the pat way Cressy was voicing it, it was obvious that this wasn't the first time that such a solution had occurred to her step-sister. She herself had never for one moment thought of contacting her mother's family. She didn't even know how to. She had heard the story of her parents' run-away marriage so often that she simply accepted it as one might a fairy story.

'Cressy, we don't know that my mother's people are wealthy. Dad could...'

'They were...they are,' Cressy interrupted her grimly. 'I've been checking up on them.' She ignored Sara's gasp of shock. 'I've been thinking about this ever since the funeral, Sara. It's the ideal solution. You can't stay in London. How could you support yourself, never mind Tom?'

'My secretarial training...'

'Oh, *that*!' Cressy brushed her stammered words aside. 'That wouldn't bring in enough to keep you both. Face it, darling, the parents used you as a drudge. You kept house for them and answered Pop's post, but that was about all. You'd never get a proper job with those qualifications. Really, darling, you don't have any alternative... You have to contact your mother's family. Look, I'll even drive you up to see them,' Cressy offered magnanimously.

'To *see* them? But, Cressy, if I do get in touch with them...surely a letter would be more...'

'Don't be ridiculous, you don't have time to get involved in letters. You need somewhere to live, Sara. Tom needs somewhere to live,' Cressy pointed out.

Tom... A tiny shaft of fear shook Sara. There were times when Tom seemed such a fragile, delicate child. She thought of him being cooped up in a tiny London bedsit, and her mouth went dry.

But what Cressy was suggesting was so...so...so calculating, she admitted unhappily. There had been no contact between her father and his first wife's family from the date of their marriage. Even after their daughter's death, they had evinced no interest in their grandchild.

'Look,' Cressy interrupted, 'what have you got to lose? What alternative do you have?'

'They might not want me,' Sara told her through stiff lips.

She missed the hard, rather unkind look her stepsister gave her.

'Well, we'll just have to make sure that they do, won't we? We'll collect Tom from school on Monday, and then I'll drive you straight up there. I might as well have Dad's car,' she added, carelessly appropriating the one asset that remained. 'You won't need it...'

Sara opened her mouth to object, and then closed it again. She felt too tired, too emotionally weary to quarrel with Cressy. Besides, she was probably right.

But the car could have been sold, a tiny voice reminded her, and that money... But there were other more important questions that demanded answers, and she voiced them uncertainly.

'Cressy, my mother's family... You seem to know so much about them...'

All her doubt and distaste of the venture her stepsister was suggesting was there in her voice, but Cressy ignored them.

'Well, one of us had to do something. Actually, Pop told me all about them. It seems they offered to take you off his hands when he and Ma married, but you were such a clinging little thing, he knew you wouldn't want to go.'

How could one describe such sensations? Sara thought wanly as she struggled to come to terms with the shock of her stepsister's revelation. She felt betrayed, abandoned, almost; she had never even known that her father had had any contact with her mother's family, that he had even been approached by them. She had always had the impression from her father that her grandparents hadn't wanted to have anything to do with her.

'Heaven knows why he didn't let you go,' Cressy said carelessly. 'And I suppose Ma would have farmed me out, too, if she could. To be honest, you'd probably have been better off if he *had* sent you to them, Sara,' she added cynically. 'They're very well off. I suppose it was always at the back of Pop's mind that he could turn to them if things ever got really desperate.'

Sara wanted to deny it, but she couldn't. She had received so many crushing blows recently and survived them, so why was it that this, the lightest of them all, should have such a paralysing effect?

She had always known that her father's love for her was at best lukewarm. If he genuinely loved any of them, it was Cressy. Cressy, who made him laugh, who flirted with him and teased him, Cressy, who was exactly the sort of vibrant daughter he would have wanted.

'It wasn't hard to get old Hobbs to do some discreet checking up,' Cressy continued.

Sara stared at her.

'You asked Dad's solicitor to do *that*?'

'Why not?' Cressy demanded carelessly, ignoring Sara's distress. 'Oh, come on!' Suddenly she was impatient and showing it. 'What other options do you have, Sara? You've always claimed to love Tom. Are you going to deny him the one chance he has of living a reasonably comfortable life? Starving in noble poverty is all very well in theory, but in practice...'

Sara knew that Cressy was right, and yet her pride recoiled instinctively from the thought of throwing herself on the mercy of the family who had so cruelly abandoned her mother. And as for Cressy's suggestion that she and Tom just turn up on their doorstep, so to speak...

'Don't you want to hear what Hobbsy found out?'

Cressy had always known how to torment her. It was almost as though she actually knew of all those lonely childhood nights when Sara had lain awake, imagining what it would be like to have a real mother, a real family. That had been before her father married Laura, of course. But, kind though Laura had been, she had never come anywhere near to filling the empty space inside her, Sara acknowledged.

It was a shock to discover that her grandparents had actually offered to have her, and even more of a shock to know that her father had kept this information from her. Why? And then, unkindly, she was reminded of how, whenever she suggested that it was time she left home to train properly for a job, her father would remind her of all the small tasks she performed which were so essential to the smooth running of the household. Tasks which no single employee could ever be asked to perform. She was allowing Cressy's cynicism to infect her, she thought miserably. Her father *had* loved her, in his way, but Cressy, being Cressy, hadn't been able to bypass an opportunity to torment her. She had always been like that. Loving and affectionate one minute, and then clawing and spitting spitefully the next. It was difficult for Sara to know what motivated her; they were such very different people.

'My little Martha,' her father had sometimes called her, and she shivered in the coldness of the unheated kitchen, remembering that the words had not always been delivered kindly.

The trouble was that she had always been too pedestrian, too ordinary to appeal to her larger-than-life parent.

'Sara, you aren't listening to me,' Cressy complained, dragging her back from the melancholy of her thoughts. 'I was going to tell you about your relatives. They live in Cheshire—your father met your mother when he was visiting Chester. Hobbsy didn't know much about their property, other than that it had been in the family for over three hundred

years.' Cressy made a face. 'God, can you imagine? No wonder your mother ran away. Your
grandmother's still alive, but your grandfather died
four years ago. Hobbsy says that your aunt and
uncle lived in Sydney, and that your cousin Louise
married an Australian. Your uncle and your cousin
were killed in a car accident over there.'

Sara sank down into one of the kitchen chairs.
Her brain felt numb, assaulted by far too much information for it to take it all in at once. She had
a family. Strange, when for so many years she had
longed and ached to know more about her mother
and her grandparents, that now that she did there
was this curious emptiness inside her.

'So that's all you've got to face, Sara. One old
lady.'

She took a deep breath and swallowed.

'Cressy, I know you mean well, but I just can't
dump myself on them...her. You must see that?'
Sara appealed frantically.

The younger girl's eyes were hard and calculating.

'So what do you intend to do? Stay here until
you're forcibly evicted? How do you think that will
affect Tom? I'm leaving for the States at the end
of the month, Sara, and nothing's going to stop
me.'

Why on earth did she feel that her stepsister had
delivered a threat rather than a warning? Sara wondered miserably, concealing her shock at the
swiftness with which Cressy had made her
arrangements.

'I can't think,' she protested. 'Cressy, I can't just go up there. I'll write to them first.'

She knew without looking at her that Cressy was furious with her. How could she make the younger girl understand that she still had her pride, that she just could not throw herself on her grandmother's charity? And yet, hours later, when Cressy had stormed out in a vicious temper, telling her that she was being criminally stubborn and selfish, she found herself standing in her father's book-lined study in front of the shelves containing all his maps and reference books.

Her hand seemed to reach automatically for what she wanted. She lifted the book down and flicked through it, stopping when she reached Chester.

She read what was written there, and tried to subdue the tiny flicker of emotion that touched her. It had been so long since she had felt anything other than weary exhaustion, that it took her minutes to recognise it as hope.

She studied a map of the county, wondering just which part of it her family inhabited. As a child, a natural reticence and over-sensitivity for the feelings of others had stopped her from questioning her father about his in-laws. She had assumed that he found talking about her mother painful, and therefore that any mention of her parents must be doubly so. And yet, apparently, he had discussed them quite freely with Cressy.

Pointless now to feel cheated, to feel that something very precious had been denied to her.

Her family had lived in the same house for three hundred years, her father's solicitor had discovered. What sort of house? Again that curl of sensation, this time aligned to a quivering inner excitement that brought a soft flush to her too-pale face.

The strain of the last few weeks had robbed her of much-needed weight. Unlike Cressy, she was not fashion-conscious, and her clothes had started to hang loosely on her slender frame. Even her hair, which was her one real claim to beauty, with its shiny, silky texture, seemed to have become dull and lifeless.

Suppose she was to write to her grandmother and that lady proposed a visit? The excitement grew. She felt like a child again, confronted with the beginnings of an especially exciting adventure. Her eyes sparkled, her air of plain dowdiness dropping away from her as hope took the place of misery.

There was no way she could do what Cressy was suggesting and simply inflict herself upon her grandmother, but a letter, explaining what could be explained without betraying her father...

The tiny seed of hope grew, and for the first time in weeks she slept peacefully and deeply.

Cressy believed in very late nights, and mornings that did not begin until close to twelve o'clock unless she was auditioning.

Sara took her a light breakfast tray at eleven, and wondered a little enviously how on earth her stepsister managed to look so good, even with most of last night's make-up still round her eyes and her forehead creased in a bad-tempered frown.

'God, my head's splitting this morning! Whoever said that you couldn't get drunk on champagne was a liar. What's this?' she demanded, grimacing as she saw the tray. 'Breakfast? Oh, for God's sake, Sara, don't be such a fool. Phone's ringing,' she added unnecessarily. 'If it's for me, take a number and say I'll ring back.'

It wasn't, and, when she had listened to the voice on the other end of the line, Sara felt that tiny seed of hope wither and die.

She walked back to Cressy's room slowly.

'Who was it?' Cressy demanded carelessly.

'Tom's school. Apparently, he had a very bad attack of asthma yesterday. Dr Robbins was very kind about it, but he feels that Tom's health is too precarious for him to continue to stay on at school. We must go and see him, Cressy—*now*!' She was shaking so much, she had to sit down, but Cressy ignored her obvious shock and said angrily, 'Now?'

It was only an hour's drive to the small, well-run prep school Tom was attending.

They were shown immediately into the headmaster's study. Dr Paul Robbins was a tall, confidence-inspiring man in his late forties and, a little to Sara's surprise and Cressy's obvious resentment, it was Sara whom he led to the chair in front of his desk, and to whom he addressed his remarks, leaving Cressy to take a very much disliked back seat.

Paul Robbins wasn't particularly impressed by pretty faces. He had enough experience of them to know they weren't worth very much without something to back them up. The pretty, pouting blonde he had recognised as one of the world's takers straight away. The other one, the quiet, hesitant girl, with the air of fragile vulnerability, she was the one who would be burdened with the care of the young boy at present lying in one of the 'San beds', being worriedly cared for by his wife.

'How is he, Dr Robbins?' Sara asked without preamble. 'Can we see him?'

'He's doing quite well now that the attack's over,' he assured her. 'And you can see him later. I wanted to have a talk with you . . . with both of you first. I'm afraid that the loss of his parents has had a very bad effect on Tom. We've taken the advice of a specialist on asthma and related problems, because this isn't the first attack he's had in the last few weeks. Of course, it's only natural that Tom should feel insecure and vulnerable at the moment, and that this vulnerability should lead to asthma attacks, but in Tom's case our specialist feels that Tom needs the security of his family around him. Some boys just do not take to a boarding-school life. Tom hasn't been unhappy here, but he has always been a little withdrawn. This withdrawal has increased since his parents' death, and we feel that, for Tom's sake, if nothing else, he would be better off at home.'

He looked down at his blotter and fiddled with his pen.

'I believe at the moment you live in London?'

The question was addressed to Sara alone, as though he was well aware that it was she and not Cressy who would bear the burden of Tom's welfare.

'Yes,' Sara agreed weakly.

He looked gravely at her. 'One of the reasons Tom was sent here to school was because it was thought that city life was not good for his health. Our specialist has corroborated that view. He feels that Tom would fare best in a quiet country environment, at least until he is old enough and strong enough to combat his asthma with other means. I don't need to tell you, I know, that he is a very frail little boy.'

Made frailer by the fact that he had received so little attention from his parents, Dr Robbins acknowledged, without saying as much. He knew quite well from his talks with Tom that it was his sister to whom the child most readily related, a sister who, by the looks of her, was almost at the end of her own fragile reserves of strength.

Sara's body tensed, her heart beating rapidly. Was Dr Robbins trying to tell her...to prepare her... He saw her face, and instantly reassured her.

'No...no, on this occasion, I assure you that he has pulled through the attack very well, but you know how weakening they are, how severely they restrict his life. Tom needs a quiet, secure background, Miss Rodney, at least for the next few years.'

He offered them tea, but Sara refused it. She was desperately anxious to see Tom and to assure herself that he was not more seriously ill than she had been told.

The little school sanatorium was bright and cheerful, but that could surely not lessen the loneliness for the little boy who was its sole occupant, Sara thought achingly as they were taken to see him.

He was sedated and drowsy with medication, but the smile he gave her made her heart turn over. He was her brother, and yet in many ways he was also her child. His parents had loved him in their careless way, but he was like her, vulnerable and in need of much more than the casual affection that was all they had time to give. She kneeled to kiss him, her throat closing up with love and fear. He was so thin, so pale, so much smaller surely than other boys his age.

They weren't allowed to stay with him for very long. Dr Robbins had arranged for them to see the specialist, who merely repeated what he had already told them. By this time, Cressy was exhibiting obvious signs of impatience and, when they were finally free to walk out to the car, she complained irately, 'Honestly, there was no need for him to go through it all again! I'm going out tonight, and now I'm going to be late.'

Sara couldn't speak. She was too shocked and worried. How could Cressy even think about going out when Tom... She bit into her bottom lip, unaware that she had torn the tender flesh until she tasted blood.

'It's just as well you've got your grandmother to turn to,' Cressy said casually as she started the car. 'There's no way you could stay in London now, is there?'

Hard eyes locked with Sara's pained, bewildered ones, and all the objections she wanted to voice died unsaid.

'I'll write to my grandmother tonight,' she said quietly, but Cressy shook her head and stopped the car.

'Sara, don't be such a fool. There isn't time for that. You heard what that fool Robbins said. He wants to get rid of Tom. He wants you to take him away. And I thought you loved him,' she added cruelly. 'If you really did, you wouldn't hesitate. Is your pride really so much more important than Tom's health?'

There was nothing Sara could say. Numbly, she shook her head, while one part of her cried out in desperation that she could not simply turn up on her grandmother's doorstep without an invitation.

She tried to reason, even to argue with Cressy, but the other girl wouldn't listen.

'Look, we'll drive down and collect Tom on Friday, and then go straight up to Cheshire.'

Sara was too exhausted to protest. All she could think of was Tom's white face; all she could hear was the specialist's dire warnings about the necessity for a quiet, secure country life.

If her grandmother wasn't wealthy, if there had been some past contact between them ... But what was the point of 'ifs'? She was caught in a situation not of her own making, and the strong sense of loyalty and responsibility bred deep in her wouldn't allow her to abandon Tom now, when he needed her most.

'Almost there.'

For the first time in weeks, Cressy sounded cheerful. Sara averted her head and stared blindly out of the window. She felt sick with nerves, desperately afraid of what was to come, and she wished she had done anything other than agree to Cressy's plans.

She had even suggested telephoning her grandmother, but Cressy had forced her to concede that a telephone call was not the best way to introduce herself to a grandmother whom she had never seen.

In the back seat, Tom was humming cheerfully. Even today, she might have found an alternative but, when they arrived at the school to collect Tom, Dr Robbins had detained her to tell her than Tom's school fees had been paid for the year, and that there would be a refund to come to her. It was as though he knew how desperately short of money they were, Sara had reflected unhappily.

By the time she got to Tom's bedside, Cressy was already sitting there, and she had been greeted with Tom's excited, 'We're going to live in the country, Sara, with your grandma, and Cressy says that I might be able to have a dog...'

Sara had been appalled. She had been literally shaking with anger and fear as she sat down on the other chair. Cressy had had no right to tell him such things! Her grandmother might turn them away, and as for a dog... She grimaced to herself. There was no way that Tom, with his asthmatic condition, could have such a pet.

All the way up the motorway, Tom had been asking eager questions about their destination. Questions which she was completely incapable of answering.

'Ah! Here's our turn-off...'

As Cressy slowed down for the motorway exit, Sara found she was actually pressing her body back into her seat, as though she could will the car to turn round and drive back down to London.

The countryside around them was flat, with hills to the east and the west. The fields were full of early summer crops, the landscape broken up by the sprawls of half-timbered farmhouses and outbuildings.

It was easy to see why this part of the country had once been so rich in arable wealth.

'Not far now...'

They drove into a small, picturesque village, and past large, turn-of-the-century houses with privet hedges and curling driveways. There were more trees here, and they grew denser as the road narrowed. Their directions had come from her father's solicitor's office, like all Cressy's information.

They approached a pair of wrought-iron gates guarded by a small, obviously empty lodge. Tom's eyes widened as Cressy turned in between the open gates.

The drive skirted a large, informal pond, green lawns stretched away into the shade of massive trees, and then Sara saw the house.

Tudor, without a doubt, it was larger than she had expected, and older. Its small, mullioned windows reflected the sunshine, and as she wound down the car window the harsh cry of a peacock made her jump.

'What's that?' Tom demanded nervously.

She told him, watching his eyes, round with excitement, as he tried to catch a glimpse of the shrieking bird.

Cressy stopped the car.

With legs that felt as though they had turned to cotton wool, Sara got out, taking Tom by the hand.

The front entrance looked formidable, a heavy oak door, closed and studded against intruders. Before she could reach for the bellpull, the door opened, and a man strode out, almost knocking her over. She had an impression of angry, dark blue eyes and a very tanned face. A firm male hand grasped her, steadying her, and just for a moment she clung to the supportive weight of his arm, aware of its strength beneath the immaculate darkness of his expensive suit.

'What the devil...' His voice was crisp, authoritative and faintly irritated. 'The house isn't open to tourists,' he told her, brusquely releasing her. 'You're probably looking for Gawsworth.'

He had already released her, and she stepped back from him, sensing his impatience. He had dark hair, very dark, and there was something about him that made her shiver slightly, some frisson of awareness that passed through her body as she watched him.

'We aren't looking for Gawsworth.'

Ah, *now* there was no impatience, Sara acknowledged, observing his entirely male reaction to Cressy's blonde prettiness. She walked towards him, all smiling confidence, sure in her ability to draw and hold his attention.

'Luke, you forgot your briefcase.'

Sara looked eagerly at the woman who had opened the door. Although well into her sixties, she was tall and upright, her silver hair immaculately groomed, her clothes elegant and understated.

This, then, must be her grandmother!

She smiled at them politely and then checked, the blood draining from her face.

'Sara ... Sara, it *is* you, isn't it?'

Sara could only nod, dry-mouthed. Her grandmother had recognised her. But how?

And then all hell seemed to break loose around her as the man turned to study her, his eyes frozen chips of winter sky, his whole body emanating dislike and contempt as he asked savagely, 'Is this true? Are you Sara Rodney?'

Too confused to speak, Sara nodded again.

Somewhere in the background she could hear Cressy speaking, her voice unfamiliar with its husky, faintly uncertain tone. Cressy had never sounded uncertain in her life. But she had forgotten that Cressy was an actress, and little chills of disbelief mingled with her shock as she heard Cressy saying uncomfortably, 'Oh, Sara, I told you you should have written first . . . I'm so sorry about this—er—Luke. But Sara insisted . . . I think she felt that she could hardly be turned away if she just turned up on your—her grandmother's doorstep. Of course, things have been hard for her lately.'

'You must come inside.'

A gentle hand touched her wrist, and Sara looked painfully into her grandmother's face.

At her side, Tom clung desperately to her hand.

'And who is this?'

'It's Tom, my half-brother . . .'

Somehow she was inside a comfortable, half-panelled hall. Rich jewel-coloured rugs glowed on the well-polished parquet floor. The room was full of the scent of beeswax, and of fresh flowers from the vases on the table.

Outside, she could still hear Cressy talking. Why was she saying those things? It had been her idea, *hers* . . . and yet now she was saying . . .

'Are you all right?'

Again that anxious, faded-blue-eyed look. Sara summoned a reassuring smile.

'A little tired. I'm sorry to arrive like this, without any warning . . .'

'My dear, I'm your grandmother. You're so like your mother—I recognized you immediately!' Tears shimmered in the pale blue depths for a moment. 'You can't know how much I've longed for this moment, how often I've imagined opening the door and finding you there. Luke...'

'I must go, otherwise I'll miss my flight.'

As the tall, dark-haired man embraced her grandmother and then looked coldly at *her*, Sara wondered what his relationship to her grandmother was. Too close to be merely a friend, to judge from the way he had embraced her. He had not struck her as a man who was free with his affections.

Out of the corner of her eye, she saw Cressy walk towards the car with him, talking earnestly to him. What was Cressy telling him? she wondered worriedly.

She knew her stepsister well enough to realise that the younger girl was hardly likely to want to paint herself in a bad light in the eyes of a personable male, and a tiny thread of fear spiralled inside her.

She dismissed it quickly. Luke, whoever he was, was not important. It was her grandmother whom she had to convince that she had come here only under duress and out of concern for Tom.

'I shouldn't have turned up like this,' she whispered as she was led into an elegantly comfortable sitting-room. How could her mother have endured to turn her back on this house of sunshine? she wondered, blinking in the golden dazzle of it as it poured in through the mullioned windows.

A portrait above the fireplace caught her eye, and she stared at it, transfixed.

'Your mother,' her grandmother told her quietly. 'Painted just before her eighteenth birthday. It wasn't long afterwards that she...she left us. Come and sit down. I want to hear all about you.' She saw the concern and apprehension cloud the hazel eyes which were so like her own late husband's, and said gently, 'Sara, something's wrong. What is it?'

How quickly and easily it all tumbled out! Her father, Cressy...and Tom. Most of all, Tom... Her love for him, and also her fear.

She badly wanted to cry, but she was so used to controlling her feelings for the benefit of others that she wouldn't allow tears to fall.

'Cressy is right,' her grandmother said when she had finished. 'You had to come here. And I'm so pleased that you have.'

Later, she would try to find out why this grand-child of hers had never responded to her constant pleas that she at least agree to see her... Her late son-in-law had a good deal to answer for, she suspected. She had never liked him, never considered him good enough for her daughter. But selfishness was not something that was restricted to other people's families, as she had good cause to know. For now, it was enough that Sara had come home. And home was where she was going to stay.

CHAPTER TWO

SHE told Sara as much over dinner, and was shocked by the look of agonised relief in her granddaughter's eyes. Alice Fitton had spent many long hours wondering about this grandchild of hers, trying to understand why it was that she had rejected their every overture of love and regret.

She had thought that Sara must be like her father: strong-willed, self-centred, uncaring of the emotional needs of others through a lack of ever having experienced them for herself. But less than half an hour in Sara's company had been enough to show her how wrong she was.

The other girl, now—Cressida... But Cressida was no concern of hers, other than that Sara seemed to be overly concerned about her welfare. Sara was speaking to her now.

'Cressy, why *don't* you stay the night?' she urged her stepsister. 'Gran is right. It's a long journey back at this time of the evening. And, besides, if you stay, it will help Tom to feel a little more settled.'

It was the wrong thing to say. Cressy frowned, an acid sharpening of her eyes and mouth dimming her normal prettiness.

'Oh, for goodness' sake, stop fussing, Sara. Tom will be perfectly all right. Anyway, I have to leave.

I have an appointment first thing in the morning, and then there's an audition for a day-time soap.'

Cressy had quickly realised that there was no way she would ever be able to charm Alice Fitton. The older woman had seen right through her, but Luke...

She smiled secretly to herself.

'I could always drive up at the weekend,' she offered tentatively.

'Oh, yes...'

Sighing faintly to herself, Alice said nothing. Perhaps she was being very uncharitable, but there was something about Cressy that she just didn't like or trust. But Sara, her heart full of happiness and relief, could only remember that if it hadn't been for Cressy's insistence she would not be here. And Cressy had been right to urge her to come; her grandmother *had* made her welcome. Already there was a rapport between them that Sara had never known with anyone else. Already she felt at home in a way she had never experienced before. Unlike her father, her grandmother did not despise her.

'After we've finished eating, I'll take you and Tom upstairs, and you can choose your own bedrooms. Luke will be pleased when he knows you're going to stay. He's always telling me I'm too old to be on my own.' The way she smiled robbed the words of any unkind intent, but Sara could not help feeling resentful on behalf of her grandmother. Who was this Luke to dare to tell her what she should and should not do?

'What's the matter?' her grandmother asked perceptively.

'Who exactly *is* Luke?' Sara asked her uncertainly.

'Of course, how could you know? Silly of me! It's just that he's been a part of the family for so long now that I forgot that you wouldn't realise. Luke Gallagher was married to your cousin Louise.'

Her cousin? Of course, Luke was the widowed husband of the cousin Cressy had told her about.

'He has very many business interests, both here and in Australia, which keep him very busy,' her grandmother sighed. 'Too busy, I sometimes think.'

It was becoming increasingly plain to Sara that her grandmother held this Luke in the greatest affection, and she was equally sure, from that one hard, encompassing look he had given her, that Luke was not going to be inclined to favour her arrival.

What her grandmother chose to do was no concern of Luke's, Sara told herself staunchly, and yet she was left with the lowering feeling that, if Luke chose to do so, he could make her life acutely uncomfortable for her. But why should he? He probably only visited her grandmother at irregular intervals, when he was in the country.

Sara didn't care for all this talk about Luke. It was making her feel acutely edgy. She didn't know why the very thought of the man had such an unwarranted effect on her; she was normally the calmest of creatures. Men had never figured very largely in her life. At twenty-three, her experience

of them was limited to the odd date, mainly with
sons of friends of her father's, young men she had
always felt uncomfortably sure had been dra-
gooned into taking her out, and for that reason she
had usually ended up tongue-tied and awkward in
their company, knowing that given the choice they
must surely have preferred to take out someone like
her stepsister.

It wasn't that she didn't like the opposite sex, it
was simply that there had never been much time
for her to get to know any of them on her own
terms.

'Well, my dear, if you really do want to leave this
evening, we mustn't delay you.'

She realised that her grandmother was inviting
Cressy to leave. She and Tom went out to the car
with her. Even though she and Cressy did not
always see eye-to-eye, she was reluctant to see her
go.

Harrison, her grandmother's chauffeur-cum-
handyman, had already removed their luggage from
the car.

'Well, with a bit of luck I'll see you both next
weekend.'

Sara stepped forward to hug her, but Cressy
moved back, grimacing faintly.

Unlike her, she had always been sparing with her
gestures of affection, especially to Tom and herself,
Sara acknowledged a little unhappily.

'I thought you were going to be busy getting
ready for your trip to America,' she reminded
Cressy, a tiny frown puckering her forehead as she

remembered her stepsister's glib explanation for the unseemly haste with which she had insisted they all come up here.

Tom had moved away from them and they were virtually standing alone. Sara felt her skin burn as Cressy taunted unkindly, 'What's wrong? Would you prefer to have Luke all to yourself, is that it?' She had driven off before Sara could make any response. She didn't usually let Cressy's bitterness upset her so much, but for some reason her final comment had made her eyes sting with hot tears.

'Come inside. It's getting quite cool. I think we'll get Harrison to light the sitting-room fire.'

There was a firm dependability about her grandmother, Sara recognised, and a gentleness that made her aware of all that she had missed in not knowing her while she was growing up. It would have meant so much to her to have this woman, this house, as a bolt-hole during the often turbulent and uncomfortable days of her teens; days when she had felt so at odds with her father and his values; days when she had felt so alone and unloved.

She knew instinctively that here she would not have experienced those feelings, and that she and her grandmother would have been attuned to one another.

'Sara, you are so different from what I'd imagined,' her grandmother commented as she led her upstairs. 'When you never replied to any of our letters——'

Sara stopped and stared at her.

'There were no letters,' she told her, shocked into unguarded speech.

'But, my dear, there *were*... Every birthday, every Christmas, at holiday time... Up until the day you were eighteen. They were sent to your father, of course.' She paused diplomatically, while Sara clung to the polished wood of the banister, trying to take in what she had just heard.

'You wrote? But...'

'But your father never told you!' Alice Fitton guessed intuitively. 'Well, perhaps he had his reasons. I must confess that there was a good deal of bitterness between him and my husband, especially when he refused to allow your mother to come home to have you... We knew how fragile she was, you see, but he insisted on taking her to Italy with him.'

'He was in the middle of his first book,' Sara whispered, her eyes dark with shock.

She had heard the story so often. How her father had been working on his first book, how he had needed to do research in Italy, and how she had been born there. She had never once heard him say that her mother had been invited to stay with her parents. Quite the contrary. Without saying so in as many words, he had nevertheless implied that his in-laws had cruelly refused to have anything to do with their daughter, even when they knew she was carrying their grandchild.

She looked into her grandmother's eyes, and knew that she was telling her the truth.

'But why?' she asked painfully. 'Why not tell me?'

'Perhaps partially to punish your grandfather and I, my dear. You see, I don't think your father ever really forgave us for not considering him the right husband for our daughter.' There was sorrow and pain in her voice, and Sara couldn't help thinking her father's resentment must surely have been fuelled by the knowledge that they were probably right. No one liked to admit that their judgement was surpassed by some other's, especially not a man like her father. But even understanding what had motivated him did not make it entirely easy for her to forgive him. It would have meant so little to him, and so much to her. She thought of all the holidays she had spent, either alone, or farmed out with friends, because her father had better things to do than to entertain a small child.

It was those memories of pain that made her so protective of Tom, she acknowledged, glancing at her half-brother now.

'Yes, he looks tired,' her grandmother agreed.

'It was for his sake that I allowed Cressy to persuade me to come here,' Sara told her. 'He suffers from an asthmatic condition that makes a quiet country life-style imperative.'

'Don't worry, Sara. This house is more than big enough to accommodate one extra child. I'm sure we shall hardly notice that Tom is here. My dear, did you really think for a moment that you would be turned away? Oh, Sara! How guilty you make me feel that we didn't try harder to make contact with you.'

Tom chose a small room with a dormer window and a sloping roof. The window looked out on to a patchwork of fields, stretching away into the purple distance of the hills.

Already he seemed happier, more relaxed, more the way a boy his age should look, thought Sara, watching him covertly.

She elected to have the room next to Tom's.

'This is mine,' her grandmother told her, indicating a further door. 'And this one is Luke's. He insists on sleeping close at hand, in case I need anything during the night.' She pulled a wry but indulgent face. 'I keep telling him that I'm far from that decrepit yet.' And then her smile faded as she turned and caught Sara's rebellious expression.

'What is it, Sara?' she asked gently. 'Every time I mention Luke's name, you almost flinch.'

'I didn't realise he actually lived here.' Sara bit her lip, aware of how breathless and nervy her voice sounded. 'I suppose it's just that I'm not used to such overpoweringly male men,' she added in a brief attempt at humor, trying to cover her obvious dismay. She didn't want to upset her grandmother by seeming to dislike a man she clearly held in high esteem.

'Yes, Luke is very male, which makes it all the more surprising...' Her grandmother broke off and grimaced faintly. 'Well, I can tell you, Sara. After all, you are my granddaughter. I'm worried about Luke. He should marry again...'

'Perhaps he prefers not to put someone else in his first wife's place,' Sara suggested gently, and earned herself a rather odd look from her grandmother. At first she thought the old lady was going to say something else, but obviously she had changed her mind, because she gave a small shrug and turned back to return downstairs.

Privately, Sara suspected there would be any number of women only too willing to fill the empty place left in Luke's life by the death of his wife, with or without a wedding ring.

Of course, she herself was immune to his brand of raw sexuality.

'Luke might be a very wealthy, very intelligent man, but he's still human, and still vulnerable,' her grandmother told her, shrewdly reading her mind. 'Let's go downstairs and have some coffee. Anna normally brings me a tray about this time.'

Anna was her grandmother's housekeeper and cook, a pretty, plump woman in her late forties.

Anna and Harrison both apparently had their own flats in the converted mews building over what had once been the stables and were now garages.

'When Luke comes back, he can show you the grounds properly. I don't walk as much these days as I used to.'

'Tell me about the house,' Sara asked impulsively when they were sitting down. Instinctively, her glance went to the portrait of her mother above the mantelpiece. Seeing it, her grandmother said gently, 'Another day, perhaps, when I can show you round, and then you'll find it more interesting.

After all,' she teased, 'it's been here for close on four hundred years—it isn't going to disappear overnight!'

'I don't know,' Sara laughed. 'It even looks like something out of a fairy-tale to me. I had no idea...'

'There have been Fittons in this part of the country for many, many years. Shakespeare even wrote about one.'

'Mary Fitton, of course,' Sara supplied, remembering the tragic story of Shakespeare's dark lady of the sonnets.

'Why don't I tell you about your mother, instead?'

'Well, if you're sure you won't find it painful...'

Her grandmother shook her head.

'No, my dear. After all, I've had over twenty-three years in which to accustom myself to the loss of your mother. Sometimes, not often, but sometimes, in my darkest moments, I wonder if it's true that the Fitton name is cursed—there have been so many small tragedies. But then your grandfather would remind me that in any family with a history stretching a long way into the past there are similar sorrows and worse.

'Your mother was a delightful child—headstrong, pretty, very like you, physically.' And although she didn't say it, she acknowledged that her daughter had had an inner light, a brightness that had either been quenched in her granddaughter or never allowed to be lit.

Now that she had the full story of the tragedy that had struck the small family, she was doubly appalled at her son-in-law's selfishness. To have made no provision for his family, especially when it contained such a young and physically vulnerable child...

'It's time I was in bed,' she told Sara with a smile. 'It's been a very exciting day for me. Don't worry about getting up in the morning.'

'You mustn't spoil me,' Sara protested. 'I ought to be thinking about what I'm going to do with the rest of my life. I should try and find out about some sort of training. I've got my secretarial qualifications. Do you think I might be able to find a job in Chester?'

'That's something we can talk about later,' she was told firmly. 'For the moment, you need to rest and relax. Goodnight, my dear.'

She had been so lucky, Sara marvelled as she prepared for bed; so much, much more lucky than she had ever dreamed she might be. That her grandmother should have welcomed both her and Tom so generously; that she should be so prepared to take them in and love them... She could hardly believe it was true.

There was only one thing to mar her happiness. Or, rather, one person.

Luke!

She shivered slightly beneath the fine linen sheets, reliving the sensation of his hands on her skin as he supported her. That he had been totally unaware of her as a woman she didn't need telling. It had been there in the brief, dismissive glance he gave her before turning his attention to Cressy.

But then that indifference had changed to a fierce, biting contempt that had blasted her fragile self-confidence, leaving her acutely vulnerable to the dislike she had felt emanating from him.

Was it just because Cressy had misrepresented her to him? She told herself that a man who could be so easily deceived by her stepsister's pretty face wasn't worth bothering about, but she couldn't dismiss him so easily.

If she stayed here, he was going to be part of the fabric of her life. Her grandmother plainly adored him. Sara was dangerously tempted to leave, but how could she? She had Tom to think about. Tom, who already seemed to have settled into his new environment.

At least Luke wasn't there all the time, if he constantly came and went on business. And if he really disliked her as much as she believed, he would be as anxious to avoid her as she was to avoid him.

So why did she feel this nagging sense of danger? Why did she find herself thinking of him as the serpent in her new-found Eden?

Although she hadn't intended to, she did oversleep. Tom woke her up, announcing that he had had his breakfast and that he was ready to explore.

'Harrison is going to show me everything,' he told her importantly.

Did Harrison know not to take him near anything furred or feathered? Anxiously, Sara got up, instructing him to stay inside until she was ready to go out with him.

She donned her usual uniform of jeans and sweater, pausing only for a moment to admire the view from her bedroom window.

Her grandmother, she learned from Anna, always had breakfast in her own room.

'It's her heart,' the housekeeper told her. 'She must rest as much as she can, but she does not always do so. Although Luke does what he can to remove most of the burden from her shoulders, there is still much work involved in organising the maintenance and running of a house such as this one.'

Listening to her, Sara made a vow there and then that she would do as much as she could to remove that burden from her grandmother's shoulders.

After breakfast, Harrison showed them round the gardens. How easy it would be to allow oneself to slip back in time here, if only in the imagination, Sara thought, marvelling at the intricacy and cleverness of a cleverly fashioned knot garden.

There was an avenue of clipped yews and quiet, shadowed pathways that led to small, secret, enclosed gardens with old-fashioned, wrought-iron benches. In one was a sundial, engraved with quotations from Shakespeare's sonnets, and in another a white-painted summer-house, shaped like a small pavilion.

How could her mother have endured to leave all this? Sara could only marvel at the power of human emotions. Had she been brought up here, could she have turned her back on it and the love of her parents to go off with a man like her father?

Perhaps it was the insecurity of her own childhood from which had grown this deep-rooted need for security. Her mother, the child of such security, might not have experienced its need quite so sharply. It was true that familiarity could breed contempt.

The gardens had such serenity, such a sense of time and timelessness. She listened as Harrison told her how each individual garden had come into being.

He had been with her parents for many years. His family came from the village, he told her. He was in his sixties, a wiry, weathered man with a quiet voice and very sharp eyes.

Tom had taken to him immediately. Like her, Tom craved security... and love.

'Do you have any dogs here?' Tom asked earnestly, and Sara quailed a little, remembering Cressy's unkind promise to him.

'Not now,' Harrison told him, shaking his head. 'We did once, but your grandmother says she's too old now for a young dog.'

They saw the peacocks and their wives, strutting beside the lake, fanning their tales in rage as humans invaded their domain. Tom stared at them in awe, fascinated by the iridescent 'eyes' in their tails.

'A present from Queen Victoria, they was,' Harrison told them, and Sara knew that he referred to the birds' original antecedents. How many stories this house must hold, how many secrets! But it lacked the brooding quality that hung like a miasma over so many old houses.

With very little imagination she could almost believe she could hear the sound of children's laughter; almost believe she could see all those long-ago children who must once have played in these gardens. As her children might, perhaps, one day play here.

It was an odd thought to have, and one that made her suddenly immensely aware of a deep inner loneliness she had been experiencing for some time.

She loved Tom and she loved Cressy. She knew she would love her grandmother as well, but Sara knew that that was not enough. She wanted to experience the same kind of love her mother must once have felt for her father; the kind of love that transcended everything else; the kind of love that was shared between a man and a woman.

Tom dragged slightly on her hand and she checked herself immediately. He must be tired, although already there was more colour in his face, a new happiness in his eyes.

'I don't know about Harrison and you, Tom, but I'm ready for some of Anna's coffee,' she said diplomatically, knowing how sensitive Tom was about his fragility.

She saw from the relief in his eyes that she was right, and that he *was* tired.

'Let's go inside, shall we?' she suggested.

'Do you know, Sara, I'm very glad we came here,' he pronounced when they were sitting at Anna's kitchen table, munching home-made biscuits and drinking coffee in Sara's case and lemonade in Tom's. 'It makes me feel sort of happy inside being here.'

Sara knew exactly what he meant.

CHAPTER THREE

FIVE days passed, a calm oasis of time, during which Sara grew to accept that she was not living in some impossible daydream, but that this was reality.

It was like watching a small, delicate flower bloom, Alice Fitton thought, watching her. She was too old now to harbour unforgiving feelings for anyone; life had taught her that it was too precious to be wasted in such fruitless emotions, but watching Sara exclaim over the beauty of a newly opened rose, seeing how hungrily she responded to every tiny gesture of affection, seeing her confidence grow almost in front of her eyes, she found it very hard indeed to understand her dead son-in-law.

By now, Sara knew almost all about the history of the house and her family; she was as familiar with its layout as her mother once must have been. She had pored over all the old family albums, and listened to most of her grandmother's stories of her own and Sara's mother's childhood.

Today, they were going to Chester. She must have some new clothes, her grandmother had insisted, and Tom, too.

They were going to have lunch at the Grosvenor as a special treat, and then, later on in the afternoon, on the way home, they were calling on some of her grandmother's friends.

Sara had demurred that she didn't need new clothes and that her existing wardrobe was perfectly adequate, but her grandmother hadn't listened, and now she and Tom were comfortably ensconced in the back of her grandmother's very old-fashioned Bentley, with her grandmother beside them and Harrison at the wheel.

There wouldn't be time on this trip to see much of Chester.

'But Luke will take you round, I'm sure. He knows almost as much about the area as your grandfather did.'

'How did he and Louise meet?' Sara asked curiously. It seemed such an odd combination, the energetic, successful Australian businessman, and a girl brought up here in this tranquil, unspoiled Cheshire countryside.

'Your uncle was very interested in farming. As you know, we don't have any land other than the gardens. He went to agricultural college, and from there to Australia, to work on one of the sheep stations there. The idea was that he would come back to this country and buy himself a farm, but while he was out there he met the woman he wanted to marry and he stayed on out there.'

'So Louise didn't actually grow up here?'

For some reason, she had imagined that her cousin must have been brought up in Cheshire, and had actually felt rather envious of her.

'Oh, no, but she did go to school over here and she spent most of her holidays with us. She wasn't like you, Sara, she didn't have your instinctive love for the house. Louise was very much a modern young woman,' her grandmother sighed. Sensing that she was reliving old, and perhaps not very happy memories, Sara quickly changed the subject.

'Your friends...'

'You'll like them. They don't live very far from us, but since I've had this little heart problem I haven't seen them as much as I should like. Gerald is confined to a wheelchair, I'm afraid—a riding accident some years ago.'

Harrison had stopped the car in the middle of a very busy shopping area. While he helped her grandmother to alight, Sara ushered Tom out of the car.

Her grandmother didn't waste time in window shopping, but instead took Sara straight into a small and, to judge from its single window, very exclusive boutique.

The assistant quite obviously knew her. Sara was introduced, and found herself being thoroughly assessed by a pair of warm brown eyes.

'What exactly are you looking for?'

'Everything,' her grandmother said before Sara could demur, and when she tried to object she was told firmly, 'My dear, please let me do this for you. Think of it as all the birthday and Christmas presents I was never able to buy you. It will give me a great deal of pleasure to see you dressed in pretty

clothes.' She looked so excited that Sara hadn't the
heart to deny her.

An hour later, as she walked out of the shop,
Sara's head was reeling. She had more clothes now
than she had ever possessed in her entire life.

Beautifully tailored linen skirts in soft, muted
pastels that did miracles for her colouring; matching
crunchy cotton knits to go with them; silky dresses
so elegant that seeing herself in them was like con-
fronting a stranger.

When she had protested that she would have no
call to wear such elegant garments, her grandmother had been almost affronted.

'Of course you will! There's Ascot, for one thing.'
And Sara had been amused to realise what a very
different world she had stepped into.

There was a tailored linen suit, a set of matching
separates, and even a very daring and, to her mind,
totally unnecessary evening dress.

'You *must* have it,' her grandmother had insisted, naming half a dozen local events for which
she insisted Sara would receive invitations.

'If I can make a suggestion,' the sales assistant
had offered before they left. 'Your hair is so very
pretty, it would be a shame to cut it, but have you
thought of copying the way the Duchess of York
wears hers?' Before Sara could object, she had pro-
duced not just a very decorative satin bow, but also
a pretty snood, into which her caught-back hair
could be tucked for special occasions.

The style suited her, revealing a delicate purity
of her features. Normally Sara didn't bother with

make-up, but today she had made a special effort, and she felt almost like a different person as she and Tom accompanied her grandmother to the Grosvenor Hotel where they were having lunch. She was wearing one of her new outfits, her hair still caught back in the style shown her by the sales assistant.

Lunch was a leisurely affair, the visit to her grandmother's friends informative and entertaining. Although of her grandmother's generation, the Armstrongs were a couple who took a keen interest in current affairs. They had a nephew apparently, who worked in Chester as a solicitor, and who was living with them while waiting for his own new house to be completed.

Tom fell asleep in the car on the way home and, rather than wake him up, Sara lifted him out of the car, ignoring Harrison's offer of help.

By the time she came downstairs, having put him to bed, her grandmother was sitting in front of the sitting-room fire, pouring them both a cup of tea.

'A most rewarding day. I like you in that colour,' she approved. 'Jeans are all very well in their place, but you have such a lovely figure, it's a shame to hide it behind those thick, bulky sweaters.'

Her grandmother didn't have a television in the sitting-room, but most evenings she went to bed at nine and then watched the news on her bedroom set. There were times when Sara wondered worriedly just how serious her grandmother's heart condition actually was. She seemed so spry and active, but sometimes in the evenings there was a

faint blue tinge to her skin, a weariness in her eyes
that tugged frighteningly at Sara's heartstrings. She
would hate to lose her now, having only just found
her.

Sara didn't mind being left on her own. A com-
panionable silence settled around her, and she
picked up the paperback book she had bought in
Chester.

Anna came in at ten o'clock to ask her if she
wanted anything. She shook her head and smiled.

'You're spoiling me, Anna,' she protested.
Shortly after that she must have fallen asleep, because the next thing she knew, she was being woken
up by someone calling her grandmother's name with
sharp anxiety.

It was dark outside, an indication of the passage
of time, only the firelight illuminating the room,
and she was too sleepily disorientated to make any
vocal response.

'Alice! Alice, are you all right?'

The voice was familiar, and yet unfamiliar in its
anxiety and concern, and then Sara froze as Luke
stepped into her line of vision.

His face registered shock and then relief, quickly
followed by contempt.

'Oh, it's you!'

'My grandmother's gone to bed,' she told him.
Her mouth had gone dry, and she couldn't stop
herself from flinching away from him. There was
something about this man that intimidated her; a
sexuality that rasped at her senses and made her all
too uncomfortably conscious of him.

Only yesterday she had been looking at photographs of him with her cousin. Even in those, he had possessed that same hardness, as though not even love was capable of softening him.

'You're still here, then?'

'My grandmother has invited me to make my home with her for as long as I wish,' she told him with dignity.

Quite clearly, her voice told him that she was not and never would be answerable to him.

'How very convenient for you. You had it all planned, didn't you—descending on her like a wide-eyed waif, clutching a child whom both you and I know very well you don't give a single damn about? Well, be warned. *I'm* not fooled by you, and if you do anything—*anything* to hurt or upset Alice, I promise you I'll make you regret it.'

Sara stared at him. What was he talking about? The very last thing she wanted to do was to hurt her grandmother.

'You know that she's very, very ill, don't you?'

The heavy seriousness of his voice tore at Sara's heart. She *had* known that her grandmother wasn't well, but Alice always made light of her condition, brushing Sara's concern aside.

'I know that she has a heart condition.'

'A very *serious* heart condition,' he stressed. 'Your grandmother is a woman I love and admire very much, and if you do anything—*anything* to hurt her...'

Mixed with her fear at his implied threat was surprise that this hard, bleak man could care so deeply
for any other human being.

Her shock must have shown in her eyes, because
he laughed harshly.

'Oh, save the injured innocent act. I know all
about you. Cressida let slip by accident what a hard
time you'd given the family. Oh, she didn't want
to tell me,' he added, looking at her with disgust.
'She's tremendously loyal to you—far more loyal
than you deserve.'

What had Cressy told him? Sara wondered
bleakly. And, more important, why?

Pride prevented her from asking him to be more
exact. It was obvious that he had formed the very
worst kind of opinion of her.

'Well, you've managed to get what you were
scheming for,' he told her curtly. 'A free meal-ticket
and a very comfortable way of life, but if I get one
hint—just *one* that you're upsetting Alice in any
way, you'll be out of here so fast...'

Much as she longed to challenge him as to his
rights to evict her from what was, after all, her
grandmother's home, Sara held her tongue. She was
getting angry now. No matter what Cressy had told
him, surely he was adult and intelligent enough to
make his own judgements?

'If you really think I'm so disreputable, why
don't you *warn* my grandmother?' she asked him
acidly instead.

'I don't want to disillusion her,' came his crisp
response. 'Your grandmother is in a very fragile

state of health. I've seen what it's done to her over the years when you've continued to ignore her overtures to you, especially since Ralph died. As I'm sure you're already well aware, it's a measure of that need that such a normally astute woman is prepared to accept your, if I may say so, risibly false change of character.'

Change of character? What on earth did he mean? Sara wondered indignantly. It was hardly her fault that her father had kept from her any information concerning her grandparents, instead allowing her to think that they had turned their backs on her.

And yet, couldn't she have pushed him a little harder, taken it upon herself to perhaps get in touch with them?

Guilt shadowed her eyes, the same guilt that had been growing in her ever since she had come here and discovered how much her grandmother loved and needed her.

How could she explain to a man as obviously strong and inviolate as this one was the very deep-seated lack of confidence that had been instilled in her at an early age? A lack of confidence that had made it impossible for her to question her father's judgements or statements.

All her life had been shadowed by the knowledge that she was not the daughter her father had wanted, she admitted unhappily. Cressy was more his idea of what his daughter should have been. Always sensitive to the feelings of others, she had known when she was quite young that he didn't love her, not as she had wanted him to love her; and she had consequently spent far too much of her life trying to measure up to the person she felt he wanted her to be.

Instinct made her turn her face into the shadows, so that Luke wouldn't see the pain reflected in her eyes.

Why did he have to live here in this house? she wondered miserably. Why couldn't he stay permanently in Australia? He loved Alice, that much was obvious, and that should have formed an immediate bond between them, but instead...

Perhaps if she'd been pretty and blonde, like Cressy, prepared to massage his ego with flattery and flirtation—and lies—he might have viewed her differently, she thought acidly.

Well, she wasn't going to let him get to her. She had as much right to be in this house as he did, she told herself sturdily, standing and facing him, her face and eyes shuttered against his hard inspection as she told him quietly, 'The relationship I have with my grandmother is private, and not something I intend to discuss with...outsiders.'

She should have felt triumph at that quickly controlled burst of rage that had flashed through his eyes, she told herself as she went upstairs, but all she could feel was a worrying frisson of fear that warned her that she was a fool to risk making an even greater enemy of such a man. But what could he really do to her? Nothing, surely?

*　　*　　*

Already, after only a few days with her grandmother, Sara had started to feel a resurgence of her
old energy, and she was downstairs—as she had
been on the previous two mornings—at the same
time as Anna, ready to help her with her morning
chores.

Sara was no stranger to domestic work. She had
run her father's household since she was in her early
teens. Laura, though never actively unkind or unpleasant to her, had never been domestically inclined, and had been more than pleased to hand
over the reins of household management to her
young stepdaughter.

Sara possessed an instinctive tact and consideration for the feelings of others, and consequently
Anna was slowly allowing her to share some of the
work. In particular, Sara insisted on preparing her
own and Tom's breakfasts, placidly pointing out
the first morning she had done this and Anna had
objected that Tom, with his asthma, required a
special diet.

This morning it was rather a shock to come down
and discover that Anna must have beaten her to it,
because the kitchen was full of the enticing smell
of freshly brewed coffee and toast. Tom was already up, for she had checked his room, so she prepared breakfast for both him and for herself and
then carried it through into the small, informal
dining-room used for that meal.

As she opened the door, she nearly dropped the
tray in her shock at seeing Luke sitting at the table,

frowning intently as he listened to Tom's earnest conversation.

A glass of freshly squeezed fruit juice stood half empty in front of the little boy, and there was a piece of half-eaten toast on his plate.

Something about the two males, so earnestly engaged in discussion, tugged at her heart strings. Her father had never had much time for the little boy. Illness of any kind frightened him, and he had never been able to admit, even to himself, that any child of his could be less than perfect. In his own way, their father had been something of a tyrant, Sara admitted unhappily. She had tried several times to tell both him and Laura that Tom needed their love and attention; that sending him away to a school no matter how excellent, was not the answer, and her view had been confirmed by the specialist Dr Robbins had called. He had told her that one of the underlying causes of the severity of Tom's asthma could be his inner insecurity.

Tom saw her first, a smile of true pleasure flashing across his thin face.

'Sara, Luke was just telling me about Australia,' he told her importantly. 'He's seen a real 'roo... That's what they call kangaroos over there,' he explained kindly to her.

There was a dazzled look of hero worship in the little boy's eyes as he turned his attention back to the now still male figure at his side; it hurt Sara deeply.

'I'm sorry if he's been bothering you,' she apologised stiffly, looking at a point somewhere above the dark head.

'On the contrary, I've enjoyed his company.' Luke got up and smiled down at Tom. 'Don't forget, young man, you and I are going on the river the first fine afternoon we get. Not all of us feel the same way about children as you do, Sara.'

What on earth had he meant by that remark? Sara wondered unhappily as he walked past her.

Anna offered to keep a quiet eye on Tom, while Sara slipped upstairs to see her grandmother. She had fallen into the habit of spending a very pleasant half-hour with her, while the older woman had her breakfast.

'Luke's back,' Alice announced as Sara walked into her bedroom. She was sitting up in bed, studying her post and, looking at her now with sharper, more worried eyes, Sara saw that she did indeed look perilously frail.

'Yes. Yes, I saw him last night.'

'He's such a marvellous man,' Alice continued happily.

'It seems rather odd that he should choose to live here when so many of his business interests are in Australia.'

'Some of them are, but not all,' Alice corrected, frowning slightly at her. 'Sara, don't you like him?'

What could she say? It was plain that her grandmother adored him, and, while she hated to lie... She bit her lip and evaded uncomfortably, 'I don't know him well enough yet to form an opinion.'

'Well, I expect you find him rather formidable. He is a very male animal,' Alice said with a chuckle. 'He reminds me very much of your grandfather when I first knew him.' She sighed, and Sara knew that she was thinking of the husband she had lost. Then her attention focused on her granddaughter, and she said softly, 'Luke is a very formidable man, I know, but he has been very, very kind to me. When your cousin died...' She sighed again, and Sara was conscious that her grandmother was remembering a very painful time in her life.

'Yes,' she agreed, trying to keep her voice scrupulously free of any shadow of her own feelings. 'It must have been a terrible blow to Luke. To lose someone you love...'

'This isn't the day to brood on past unhappiness,' her grandmother chided her. 'Luke told me this morning that it will be some time before he needs to go abroad again. We're a little bit remote here, and I must confess that I always feel more at ease when he's at home. Your stepsister is due tomorrow, isn't she?'

'She did say she might visit,' Sara agreed. She felt reluctant to see Cressy. There was an angry resentment inside her that her stepsister could have lied to Luke about her. Cressy had always been adept at tailoring the truth to meet her own requirements, but Sara had never guessed that she would actually lie.

And why? She knew that Cressy always wanted people to see her in a good light, and Luke was exactly the type of man to appeal to her stepsister, but what could she possibly have to gain in lying about *her*?

'You don't sound very happy, my dear. Is something bothering you?'

'Only the extravagantly large amount of money you insisted on spending on me yesterday,' Sara fibbed.

'My dear...' Alice broke off as someone knocked on her door.

Sara's muscles froze as Luke walked in. She made to get up and go, but her grandmother motioned her to stay.

'Luke, I was just telling Sara that she mustn't mind me spoiling her,' she announced.

'Spoiling her?'

A narrow-eyed gaze pinned her guilty flesh.

'Oh, just a few new clothes,' Sara heard her grandmother explaining, oblivious to the undercurrent of hostility flowing between the two of them. 'The poor child was desperately short of decent things to wear.'

'Strange,' Luke mused, his eyes hard and watchful, waiting to trap her, Sara thought, panicked by the menacing intent of them. 'I'm sure Cressida mentioned to me that you'd been given almost an entire wardrobe of designer clothes by a...*friend*.'

Sara could scarcely believe her ears. The person who'd received the designer clothes had been Cressida herself, and that had been during a rather dubious relationship she had had with a man involved in the media. Cressy had hoped, through him, to break into the extremely lucrative world of TV advertising.

Cressy had told her about the clothes in an unguarded and boastful moment, when she had been unkindly comparing what she termed as the 'drudge' of a life that Sara led and her own.

'Sara?'

Sara realised that her grandmother was looking at her with puzzled curiosity.

'I think Luke must have misunderstood,' she said tightly, her face flaming with hot, angry colour. Part of her was furious that he should choose to attack her in this way, and the other part shrank from revealing the truth. She had always had a very strict sense of honour, but she couldn't allow his remark to go unchallenged. 'In actual fact, *Cressy* was the one who received the designer clothes. She's an actress, you know, and I think she got them in lieu of payment for some work she did.'

She hoped her statement was bland enough not to provoke any more questions, but she suspected, from the shrewd look in her grandmother's eyes, that the older woman had guessed at much of what had been left unsaid.

Luke waited until they were both well away from her grandmother's bedroom before attacking her again. She had excused herself and left quickly, hoping to avoid him, but he caught up with her on the stairs, grabbing hold of her so roughly that she winced beneath the pressure he was exerting.

She didn't like being so close to him; close enough to see the faint shadow where he shaved, and the anger-darkened irises of his eyes.

For a businessman, he was unusually fit, she decided unsteadily, horribly aware of how much physically stronger than her he was.

'Very clever,' he snarled at her. 'Laying the blame on your stepsister... Alice believed you this time, but believe me, she won't always be so easy to deceive. At the moment, she's caught up in the euphoria of finding a granddaughter who is so almost exactly what she's always wanted, so she isn't functioning in her normal, astute fashion, but that euphoria won't last for ever.'

Why was he so protective of her grandmother? After all, it wasn't as though there was any blood relationship between them. And then she remembered Alice saying that he had been orphaned as a child, and had grown up virtually alone.

'You're jealous,' she breathed triumphantly. 'You're jealous because my grandmother loves me!'

'Why, you...'

For a moment, Sara thought he was actually going to throw her down the stairs, and in her panic she clung desperately to the lapels of his jacket, her whole body tensing in fear.

'My, my, darling! I always knew you were a quick worker...'

Sara hadn't heard the door open. Her head swivelled round, and she stared down into the hall. Cressy was standing there, her blue eyes sharp with malice.

'I didn't expect you to arrive so early,' she said stupidly, unaware that she was still clinging to Luke's jacket, or that he was still gripping her shoulders.

He released her so abruptly that she practically fell.

'Your sister's come a long way to see you, Sara,' he told her abruptly. 'Surely the least you can do is to make her feel welcome.'

Open-mouthed, Sara watched as he went downstairs to greet Cressy, upset by the shaft of resentment she had felt when she looked down and saw her stepsister looking up at them.

She had never resented Cressy in the past, accepting the fact that she was more in tune with her father than *she* was ever likely to be, so why on earth was she resenting her now?

Because she had lied about her to Luke? What did it matter what he thought of her? And surely she was confident enough of her grandmother's affection not to fear that she would believe anything either Cressy or Luke said to her?

So then, why?

CHAPTER FOUR

IT WAS gratifying to find her judgement supported later in the day when her grandmother confided to her, 'I know Cressy is your stepsister, my dear, but I really cannot like her.' She sighed and looked concerned. 'In many ways, she reminds me of your cousin.'

'Luke's wife?'

'Yes. She had that same blonde delicacy that can be so deceptive, and so often hides a will of steel. They share the same innate selfishness as well, I suspect.'

Sara knew that her grandmother was referring obliquely to the fact that, although Cressy had purportedly come to Cheshire to see Tom and herself, she had in actual fact persuaded Luke to drive her to Chester, claiming that she had forgotten to bring her suitcase and therefore needed to buy one or two things.

Sara hadn't been sorry to see the pair of them leave. Luke spoiled the tranquillity of her grandmother's home for her. She felt constantly on edge in his presence. She would have liked to have been able to talk to her grandmother about Luke's misjudgement of her but, knowing how much she thought of him, Sara hesitated to disillusion her.

If Luke wanted to believe Cressy's fibs, then let him. She suspected he had judged her even before he had met her; and in fairness she had to admit that, given the fact that he was not aware of her reasons for not getting in touch with her grandparents before, on the face of it he did have a good basis for his contempt. But only a basis. Surely he could have given her some small benefit of doubt?

In her view, though, that did not alter the fact that he could have been less hostile towards her; he could, in fact, as her grandmother had done, have invited her to confide in him.

Oh, what was she doing, wasting a beautiful afternoon thinking about him? she derided herself.

She had learned that her grandmother was supposed to rest far more than she did, and she suggested diplomatically now that she take Tom out of her way for an hour or so.

His asthma attack behind him, Tom was now as energetic as any other eight-year-old, all the more so in fact, Sara suspected, through having been used to the quite strict discipline of his boarding-school.

She found him in the kitchen, looking rather downcast, and asked him what was wrong.

'Luke promised to take me fishing this afternoon, and now he's gone out with Cressy instead.'

'Well, I'm sure he'll take you another time,' Sara offered palliatively, while mentally condemning Luke's thoughtlessness in breaking his promise to Tom. It was reassuring to realise that Luke was not as perfect as he liked to believe.

'Perhaps you could take me instead,' Tom suggested, brightening slightly.

Sara wished she could, but she knew next to nothing about the sport, and so regretfully she shook her head.

It was very much later, in the evening, before Cressy and Luke returned. Her grandmother had not said anything, but Sara had sensed her disappointment when they did not return for dinner, and her own anger had grown.

Cressy's selfishness was something she was accustomed to, but for some reason she had expected better of Luke. He must have known surely how much her grandmother was looking forward to his company?

For someone who so quickly and damningly set himself up in judgement on others, he had a very lax attitude indeed where his own behaviour was concerned!

All evening, Sara's anger had been growing. She was in the kitchen, washing the supper things, when they returned. It was Anna's evening off, and she saw the sweep of Luke's headlights as he drove the car into the garage.

She was just walking through the hall when they came in, Cressy flushed and laughing, her small, satisfied cat's smile very much in evidence as she clung to Luke's arm.

'Heaven's, Sara, what on earth are you doing there?' she demanded when she saw Sara pausing at the foot of the stairs. 'Lying in wait for us?'

'I was just on my way to bed,' Sara told her, smothering her distaste.

'Oh, but I wanted to talk to you.'

'Can't it wait until morning? I'm rather tired.'

'Whoops! I think she's sulking, don't you, Luke?'

Sara was furious. It was one thing for Cressy to goad her like this in private, quite another to do it in front of Luke.

'I am *not* sulking, Cressy,' she retaliated quietly. 'If you and Luke choose to spend your time together, that's entirely your affair. However, I do think,' she paused and looked directly at Luke, 'that you might have considered at least warning other people what you intended to do, especially when you'd already made prior commitments...'

'What sort of prior commitments?' Cressy demanded sharply, looking from Sara's white, angry face, to the dark, set one of the man at her side.

'Goodnight, Cressy,' Sara told her firmly.

She was shaking when she walked into her bedroom. She hated rows of any kind, but tonight she had been so furious... Her nails dug into the soft palms of her hands. A warm bath would help to relax her, and she was just pulling on her robe for the trip to the bathroom when her bedroom door opened.

She had her back to the door, but instantly she tensed. The last thing she wanted now was a confrontation with Cressy.

'Not now, Cressy,' she said tiredly. 'We'll talk in the morning.'

'Oh, no, we won't—we'll damn well talk *now*!'

The unexpected male voice grated against already raw nerves. Sara spun round, gaping at Luke as he determinedly closed her bedroom door.

'You can't walk in here like that! This is *my* room...'

He ignored her shocked protest, walking towards her, his eyes and mouth bitter.

'Now, perhaps you'd be kind enough to explain that remark you made downstairs. And don't try pretending that it *wasn't* directed at me. I know that it was. What promises am I supposed to have broken, and to whom?'

'Tom,' she told him huskily, her chin tilting as she braved the inimical look he was giving her. 'You promised to take him fishing.'

'This weekend. Yes, I did. But the weekend isn't over yet...'

Sara felt her face flame with a mixture of chagrin and temper.

'Tom thought you meant this afternoon. And Grandmother expected you back for dinner.'

'I fully intended to be back, but circumstances dictated otherwise.'

'Oh, yes. Too busy getting Cressy to tell you all about my murky past to remember the time, were you?'

Sara was horrified with herself. No one had ever provoked her to such rashness before.

'Why, you...'

She panicked as he caught hold of her, terrified by the violence she could see in his eyes. She kicked out at him wildly, frantic with primeval terror as she felt the strength in his hands. He could break her neck as though it was nothing more than a matchstick.

'Stop it! Stop panicking.' The anger in his voice only served to increase her fear. She lashed out wildly, almost as shocked as he was when her hands made contact with his skin.

There was a faint red mark along his jaw where the blood throbbed angrily, and she couldn't drag her terrified gaze away from it.

Almost as though it was happening in slow motion, she heard Luke's feral snarl and caught the furious glitter of his eyes. His grip had changed somehow, and he had pinned her arms out of the way, so that she had no way of stopping the downward descent of his head.

She knew instinctively how he was going to punish her, and at the last moment tried to turn her head aside in frantic horror, but his hand cupped it, inflicting such pressure on her jaw that she couldn't move without causing herself pain.

The hard, angry pressure of his mouth was every bit as punishing as she had feared. She started to tremble violently and, as though her fear excited his anger, she felt the pressure of his mouth increase.

Sara had never been kissed like this, and every sense she possessed reacted to what she was experiencing. Luke shifted his weight somehow, so that she fell heavily against him. She could feel the hard imprint of his body against her own, in angry defilement. She wanted to move away, but she couldn't. She made a small, whimpering sound of protest beneath his mouth that echoed her confusion and shock, but, when she tried to evade him, his teeth nipped warningly at her bottom lip.

She had heard of people being kissed like this, in anger and retaliation, but she had never imagined she would experience it. And then, shockingly, an odd lick of warmth began somewhere deep inside her, spreading insidiously through her veins. Her lips, ignoring the furious protest of her brain, softened as though in enjoyment of the fierce pressure caressing them, her body tensed, her eyes widening in shock.

Instantly Luke froze, pushing her away from him.

There was a dark stain of colour high upon his cheekbones, and his eyes were almost black. He stared at her, with an ugly smile twisting his mouth, his chest heaving as though he had been running.

'Oh, no! I'm too old and too experienced to fall for that one,' he told her brutally. 'Finding your celibate life up here a bit of a strain, are you?'

His immediate awareness of her tentative response humiliated her beyond measure—sullying the sweetness of that unbidden reaction, but at least he didn't realise that it was he himself who was responsible for it, rather than just an instinctive sexual need.

'Get out of here!' she spat the words at him in a low whisper that throbbed with the force of her emotions.

When he had gone, all she wanted to do was to curl up somewhere and die. She caught a glimpse of herself in the bedroom mirror and hot colour warmed her skin again as she saw the clearly discernible pointed thrust of her breasts pushing against the fine cloth of her blouse.

Physical arousal! It was not something with which she was overly familiar. A new and very unpleasant thought struck her. She wasn't *jealous* of the fact that Cressy had spent the day with him, was she? Her anger had only been motivated by the fact that Luke had forgotten his promise to Tom, hadn't it?

Anna didn't work on Sundays, and Sara had already told Anna that she was quite happy to take over her chores.

She got up early, dressing casually in her jeans and a cool cotton top, since the day looked like being fine. Downstairs, she set about preparing breakfast trays for her grandmother and Cressy. Tom was still in bed, and so she had time to organise the table in the small dining-room.

There was a joint of beef in the fridge for lunch. She stopped what she was doing, not seeing the view beyond the kitchen window, but remembering instead Sundays in London when her father and Laura had been at home.

They had invariably invited a large crowd on Sundays. Sara had been instructed to prepare some food. Her father always had what looked like an endless supply of wine. The conversation had been

witty and urbane, and yet she had never felt relaxed or comfortable with her father's friends.

Luke walked in just as the coffee had finished
perking. He looked surprised to see her.

'It's Anna's day off,' she told him by way of explanation, her nerves jumping as he came too close
to her.

He gave her an irate look.

'Yes, I know.'

He was dressed casually in jeans and an open-
necked, short-sleeved white shirt. Sara could feel
herself blushing as her glance inadvertently lingered
on the muscled stretch of his legs.

She knew he was watching her, and she could
well imagine the derision that would be in his eyes.
What was the matter with her, for goodness' sake?
She had seen men wearing a well-fitting pair of
jeans before. Many of them, in fact, but it was an
unpalatable truth that none of them had had the
effect on her that this man was having.

'If you want to go through to the dining-room,
I'll bring in your breakfast.' All her dislike and
mistrust of him showed in her voice.

'*You're* making breakfast?'

His incredulous query checked her, her eyebrows
lifting slightly as she told him briskly, 'Yes, I am.'

He looked even more incredulous minutes later
when she served him with a perfectly cooked
English breakfast. He was probably wondering if
she had put poison in it, Sara thought wryly,
watching him from beneath demurely lowered
lashes. If only she had!

He took a bite, and said grudgingly, 'It's good.'

Sara smiled sweetly at him and replied, 'I believe arsenic always takes some time to take effect,' and then she turned on her heel and left, going upstairs to wake Tom.

'Luke's been in to see me,' Tom announced importantly, sitting up in bed and beaming at her. 'He's taking me fishing this afternoon.'

Well, she just hoped he stuck to his promise this time, Sara thought darkly as she urged Tom to get up.

A quick peep into her grandmother's room showed her that she was already awake, although, when she looked in on her stepsister, Cressy was still deeply asleep.

Luke came back into the kitchen as she was preparing her grandmother's tray. Sara was surprised to see that he had carried out his own used dishes. Her father would never have dreamed of doing anything so domestic.

'Who are these for?' He looked at the two prettily arranged trays.

'Gran and Cressy.'

'Cressy?' His glance sharpened, a slight frown furrowing his forehead.

'Yes, do you want to take it up for her?' she asked him evenly. She had promised herself last night that all this nonsense in the way she was reacting to him had to stop. She must accept, as she had thought she had already taught herself to accept, that Cressy was the type of woman who appealed to men, and she was not.

Cressy was like Louise, her cousin, or so her grandmother had said. Naturally, Luke would be drawn to a woman who was similar to the wife he had loved and lost.

'What exactly are you implying?' he asked her coldly. 'That your stepsister and I are lovers?' His unexpected attack puzzled her until he said softly, 'Cressy warned me that you would probably try to discredit her in the eyes of your grandmother. She says you're very good at playing the role of the hard-done-by little Cinderella.'

A hard lump of pain lodged in her throat, almost choking her. How could Cressy have spoken about her like that?

'How despicable you are, Sara, playing on an old woman's very natural yearning for the grand-child she had never known; the only grandchild she had left. No wonder your father tied up his money so that you can't touch it. Oh, yes. Cressy told me why you were so determined to hold on to Tom! I know that she offered to take him to California with her, but of course you couldn't afford to let him go, could you? If you did, you would lose the income that comes from the trust your father set up—an income which is only payable to whichever of you looks after Tom.'

Sara was stunned—and then very angry! What on earth had Cressy told him?

'I'll take *Alice's* tray up,' he told her grimly. 'And don't worry, Sara. I'm not going to tell her the truth about her dearly loved grandchild—for her sake, not yours.'

He was gone before she could find the breath to deny his allegations. Allegations that were based on the web of lies Cressy had spun for him.

Sara waited until she was sure Cressy would be awake before going to see her stepsister.

Cressy frowned when she walked in, waving away the breakfast tray.

'God, you know I hate food in the morning,' she said petulantly. 'What time is it? I want Luke to take me somewhere decent for lunch. What a hole this place is! I don't know how you can stand it...'

'Cressy, what have you been telling Luke?' Sara interrupted quietly.

It hurt her to see the evasion in Cressy's eyes, and she knew that she had been right in suspecting that her stepsister had lied to Luke about her.

She said as much, and Cressy didn't attempt to deny it, shrugging and then yawning with bored indolence.

'Oh, for goodness' sake, Sara, grow up. Luke is an extremely rich man. I want to marry him.'

'Marry him?' Sara goggled at her. This was the last thing she had expected to hear. Cressy had never made any secret of her contempt of the married state. 'But your career...'

'Will flourish much better once I have a wealthy and influential husband to support me.'

'But you were doing so well. You were going to California...'

'*Were* being the operative word,' Cressy told her acidly. 'The California thing's off. I'm broke, Sara, and I need to marry Luke... Once I've got my career established, I can ditch him, of course.' She shrugged again, patently indifferent to Sara's shocked response to her disclosures.

Why, when he had treated her so badly, did she feel acutely sorry for the man? Sara wondered soberly. She had always known that Cressy was self-centred, but she had never dreamed that her step-sister would go to these lengths.

'I still don't understand,' she protested. 'Why discredit me?'

'Oh, just to make sure you aren't any compe-tition. Wise up, darling,' she said mockingly. 'A man like Luke enjoys protecting what he still idi-otically believes to be the weaker sex. How do you think it's felt for me all these years, Sara, with you constantly held up in front of me as some sickening model of perfection. I must confess, when I first suggested you come here, it was just so that I could get you and Tom out of my hair. But it's turned out even better than I imagined.' She gave a small gurgle of laughter. 'Honestly, you wouldn't believe how pathetically eager Luke is to believe the worst of you. Seems he blames you for not getting in touch with your grandparents before now. Of course, I haven't done anything to disillusion him, and neither must you, darling.'

The faint purr of a threat entered the last few words. Sara stared at her stepsister in dismay. This was a Cressy she hadn't known existed, and she could only listen to her disclosures in shocked silence.

'Luke, although he doesn't know it, is very vulnerable,' Cressy continued, smiling at her. 'He's a man to whom the idea of marriage and a family has an intense appeal. He's also the old-fashioned sort,' she added shrewdly. 'Oh, I'm not saying he hasn't had his moments,' she admitted frankly. 'No man as physically attractive as he is couldn't have done. All I have to do is to convince him that I need his protection, and to do that, what better than to adopt your poor little "Martha" role, my dear?'

'Cressy, you can't mean any of this!' Sara objected painfully.

'Oh, but I do, and don't get any stupid ideas in your head about warning Luke of what's in store for him. He won't believe you, you know.'

Sara knew Cressy was telling the truth. Luke would never believe anything she might have to say, still less any wild and apparently impossible claims she might make about Cressy's determination to marry him.

'Cressy, please think,' she implored. 'He's already been hurt once...'

'Oh, dear, you're not falling in love with him, are you, darling?' Cressy gave a malicious trill of laughter as she delivered the gibe.

Sara denied it instantly. Of course she wasn't falling in love with the man! She disliked him just as much as he disliked her!

Thoroughly infuriated by Cressy's taunt, Sara went back downstairs. She told herself that she ought to be highly delighted that Luke was going to get his come-uppance, but somehow she wasn't!

She tried to concentrate pleasurably on his re-action when he discovered that Cressy had married him merely for his wealth and as a means to pro-moting her career but, instead of pleasure, all she could feel was dismay. Dismay on Luke's behalf. She must be going mad.

She knew her stepsister well enough to know Cressy hadn't lied when she said she would ulti-mately leave him. Cressy would never commit herself to another human being. She didn't have that sort of personality. She was completely dedi-cated to her own future success.

Despite the fact that Sara had taken immense pains with it, Sunday lunch was not a success.

There was nothing wrong with the food, but Cressy sulked all the way through the meal because Luke had refused to take her out somewhere. Sara could see that her stepsister's snide, bitter remarks were causing her grandmother to look tired and strained.

Only Tom seemed to be relaxed as he bubbled over with excitement about the afternoon's planned fishing.

They owned a small stretch of river locally, her grandmother explained to Sara once the two males had gone, Tom carefully protected against the water with his wellingtons.

Although she was trying not to show it, she was anxious about Tom's welfare. What if something should happen while they were out to bring on one of his attacks?

'Stop worrying,' her grandmother chided her gently. 'Tom is in the best of hands. Luke will take proper care of him.'

Cressy was still sulking, and had retired to her room with some glossy magazines Luke had bought her in Chester.

She had announced to Sara that the West End play she was in would be closing at the end of the month, and Sara suspected that she fully intended to inveigle either Sara or Luke himself to invite her to stay on in Cheshire.

Sara was in a quandary. The old habit of loyalty died hard, and Cressy *was* her stepsister. On the other hand, it was plain that her grandmother didn't like her and, in her delicate state of health, Sara felt she owed it to Alice to keep them apart.

The Armstrongs arrived later in the afternoon, having been driven over by their nephew, who turned out to be a very pleasant young man, several years older than Sara.

Andrew was an entertaining raconteur, with a fund of stories about various cases in which he'd been involved, while working in London. Sara discovered that they shared a love of chamber music and the Victoria and Albert Museum, and the afternoon seemed to fly past.

It was five o'clock before Luke and Tom got back, Tom bursting with pride as he told them of the tiddlers he had caught. 'We had to throw them back, though,' he told Sara seriously. 'Luke said they had some more growing to do yet, and that it wasn't fair to kill them.'

Already his appetite had improved, Sara noticed, remembering how before it had sometimes been necessary to coax him to finish a meal.

Cressy was leaving after they had eaten. Listening to her conversation with Luke, Sara realised that she was still preserving the fiction of going out to California. No doubt she hoped to push him into committing himself to her with the threat of her absence, Sara acknowledged cynically.

She wasn't surprised to hear them making plans to meet in London during the week, but what did surprise her was her own reaction to it.

There was no reason at all why she should feel so hurt by Luke's continued misjudgement of her; rather, she should feel contempt for him in his inability to see past Cressy's pretty face.

She went upstairs with Cressy to help her pack, and was stunned when the other girl turned on her and said vitriolically, 'Don't think I don't know what's going on! Your grandmother's trying to pair you off with Luke.' She laughed acidly, and Sara was struck by the unpleasantness of the sound. 'He wouldn't look at you in a month of Sundays.'

Was her grandmother trying to pair her off with Luke? Surely not? Surely she was far too sensible? But she was also a very frail lady, from a different generation; a generation when families had had far more influence over the partners their children chose. Sara already knew how much her grandmother thought of Luke. But surely she must see how ill-suited they would be? Why, every time he came to within speaking distance of her, she could feel her muscles tense. He despised her, and she disliked him. But she had an unwary memory of that brief softening of her lips while he'd inflicted his harsh punishment on her, and a fine shiver of unfamiliar sensation tracked across her sensitive skin.

'I hardly know why Cressida bothered to come up here,' Sara heard her grandmother remarking mildly, once she had gone. 'She didn't spend much time at all with Sara, or Tom.'

'Perhaps because she wasn't given the chance to,' Luke retorted in a clipped voice. He looked across at Sara, his eyes cold and hard as he added, 'I feel it was rather unkind of you to refuse to allow Cressy to borrow any of your new clothes. It would only have been for a couple of days.'

Sara refused to try to defend herself, although she could have hugged Tom when he turned to Luke with a puzzled expression in his eyes and said uncertainly, 'Why would Cressy want to wear Sara's clothes? She says they're nothing but rags and fit for the dustbin.'

Cressy *had* said something of the sort, but Sara hadn't realised that Tom must have overheard her.

There was a small, uncomfortable silence, during which Tom looked worriedly from Sara's quiet face to Luke's hard one.

'Can we go fishing some other time?'

His voice quavered slightly, just as it used to when he tried to engage their father's interest, Sara recognised. She waited, tense with dread that Luke

might reject him, expelling her pent-up breath only
when Luke said quietly, 'I don't see why not.'

'I think it's time you were getting ready for bed,'
Sara inserted. 'Why don't you say goodnight, and
then go up and get ready?'

'And then will you come up and tell me a story?'
He looked at Luke and told him proudly, 'Sara tells
really exciting stories...'

She ought to have been pleased by the frown that
furrowed the tanned forehead. She could see that
Luke was puzzled by the rapport between Tom and
herself. No doubt it didn't fit in with the picture
Cressy had drawn for him. Well, she wasn't going
to make any explanations, she decided fiercely.

It was only when she was upstairs, pulling the
sheet up round Tom as he fell asleep that she admitted to herself that, for a man she was supposed
to despise and dislike, Luke was occupying far too
many of her thoughts.

She wished he would go back to Australia and
stay there, she decided despairingly as she walked
back into the sitting-room.

Luke was sitting next to her grandmother. Both
of them looked up as she walked in.

'Tom is very lucky to have you, my dear,' her
grandmother praised her warmly. 'He's such an attractive child. It's a pity about his asthma.'

'There's every chance that he might grow out of
it,' Sara defended automatically, a quick flush
colouring her skin as she caught her grandmother's
surprised look.

She hadn't been criticising Tom, Sara recognised, but she was so used to her father's unkind attitude to the little boy that she had instinctively rushed to his defence.

'I was just telling Luke that he must take you to the Midsummer Ball. It's a charity "do" that's held at the Grosvenor. A most wonderful affair. You'll thoroughly enjoy it.'

Sara couldn't look at Luke; she knew how little he would want to escort her to such an affair. Her head bent as she mumbled the first excuse that came to her mind, a guilty flush staining her skin.

It was wrong to pretend that she couldn't leave Tom, but there was no way she was going to endure the humiliation of listening to Luke find an excuse for not accompanying her.

It was plain that her grandmother was disappointed, and Sara felt guilty at spoiling her happiness. *Was* her grandmother entertaining foolish dreams of a marriage between Luke and herself?

If so, she would have to find a way of making her see how impossible they were, Sara acknowledged.

CHAPTER FIVE

As she surveyed the flowerbed she was weeding, Sara eased her aching back with a small smile of satisfaction.

She had been living with her grandmother for over a month now, but it was only this week that she had discovered the pleasures of gardening. She was weeding one of the intricately planted knot gardens, and it was almost idyllic work, kneeling in the full strength of the summer sun, breathing in the clean smell of the earth and the scents of the flowers.

Tom had made friends with a couple of boys in the village, and he was out with them now, riding his bicycle. The bicycle had been a present from Luke—a very generous present, Sara admitted.

In Luke, Tom was finding the guidance and firmness he had never received from their own father. Luke would be a marvellous parent.

He had been to London several times to see Cressy, and as far as she knew her stepsister was still preserving the fiction that she was going to California, although her departure had been delayed.

Only last weekend Cressy had asked her for money, complaining that she was completely broke. Sara had given her what little she had. Her own bank account was practically depleted, and she was too proud to ask her grandmother for any.

She had decided that she would have to find a job, locally if possible, if not, in Chester. She was gradually taking over more and more responsibility for the house, and thus relieving her grandmother of its burden. She frowned as she plucked at a recalcitrant and deep-rooted weed.

Her grandmother was shortly due to visit her specialist in London. Every time Sara tried to raise the subject of her health, she evaded her questions. There was no doubt in Sara's mind now that her grandmother was far more frail than she wanted anyone to think. She glanced at her watch. Three o'clock. Time to go in and have a cup of tea.

She went first to the kitchen to wash her hands, and then to take the tray from Anna.

She pushed open the sitting-room door, calling out cheerfully, 'Tea and Anna's scones!' and then almost dropped the tray as she saw her grandmother's crumpled figure.

She put down the tray with shaking hands, calling frantically for Anna.

Her grandmother was still alive. She could feel her pulse-beat, but her colour was frightening and her breathing so shallow.

'Anna, please call the doctor...'

She didn't know how she managed to get the words out of her choked throat. All the time, a message was beating through her brain. She mustn't panic...she mustn't panic... If only Luke was here...a small sob caught in her throat, and she suppressed it.

'Perhaps we should carry her upstairs,' Anna suggested.

'No, no!' Sara said sharply. 'We'd better not touch her. She might have broken something when she fell, Anna,' she added more gently.

The doctor seemed to be a lifetime in arriving, although it could only in fact have been minutes. Sara prayed as she had never prayed before that her grandmother would live.

The doctor's examination was quick and knowledgeable. He popped a tablet into her grandmother's mouth and then said to Sara, 'She's been lucky this time. I've warned her time and time again against overdoing things.'

'How...how serious is it?'

'Serious enough,' he told her gravely. 'She's starting to come round. I'll take her upstairs. Could you come with me?'

When her grandmother finally came round, Sara was sitting on her bed, holding her hand, her face anxious.

'Gran...' Her voice broke, and she stifled the tears burning her eyes.

'It's all right, my dear.' She patted Sara's hand. 'I have these little turns from time to time. Don't I, Doctor?' she appealed to the man standing beside the bed.

'Only when you don't do as you're told,' he asserted firmly.

To hear her grandmother's chuckle was such a relief.

'You frightened me,' Sara told her unsteadily.

It was shock that was making her tremble so badly, Sara acknowledged, as she fought to control the tremors in her hands.

'Oh, my dear!'

Sara saw the concern in her grandmother's eyes, and fought to get herself back under control.

'You're to stay in bed for the rest of the day,' Sara heard the doctor telling her. 'You're due to see Alan Gray soon, aren't you?'

'Yes, next week,' her grandmother agreed placidly.

'Um...well, take things easy until then.'

Sara saw him out to his car.

'Try to make sure she rests,' he urged her.

'Is there anything I can do?'

He gave her a kind smile.

'No, my dear... Just having you here is the best medicine she could have, but she must learn that she has to take things easy. She can get up later, if she wants to.'

'Sara, promise me you won't say anything about this to Luke.' She was upstairs with her grandmother. It was some time since Alice's accident, but Sara still felt shaky.

'I don't want him to worry,' her grandmother persisted, seeing the doubt in her eye.

'All right, I won't tell him,' Sara agreed reluctantly.

Luke was away in London, and not due back until very much later in the evening. She *ought* to tell him about Gran, Sara acknowledged later that evening. She could understand that Gran didn't want to worry him, but the seriousness of her condition was such that Sara didn't think she had the right to keep it from him.

She would wait up until he came home and tell him, Sara decided. And then she remembered that her grandmother sometimes couldn't sleep and came down to make herself a drink or get a book. If she discovered her down here, she was bound to guess that she was waiting for Luke—and why.

It would be better if she waited for him in his room.

Sara had never been in Luke's room before. It wasn't very far from her grandmother's, and she opened the door with a faint feeling of trepidation.

She had been in the middle of getting ready for bed when she had been forced to acknowledge that she would have to break her promise to her grandmother and tell Luke what had happened, and she had pulled on an old terry-towelling robe over her underclothes.

She had brought a book with her, but she was too strung up with adrenalin-based tension to pay much attention to it. She read a half a dozen words, and then the print blurred and all she could see was her grandmother's still form.

She looked at her watch. Luke normally got back about eleven, and it was now almost ten past. She stifled a yawn. Her body ached from her gardening

stint this afternoon, and her head was beginning to
feel muzzy. She yawned again and looked yearn-
ingly at the bed.

Luke's room had a very traditional four-poster.
In fact, all the furniture in the room was very old
and very valuable. It was decorated in rich shades
of blue and terracotta. Anna had turned down the
bed invitingly.

She looked at her watch again. Half-past eleven.
When would Luke be back?

At one o'clock she gave in to the tiredness that
was making her head muzzy and her body ache,
and crawled on to a shadowy corner of the bed.

She fell asleep almost immediately, unaware of
the bright arc of Luke's car's headlights, or of his
entry into the house.

Not even the sound of the shower in the adjacent
bathroom had the power to wake her, and so the
first thing she knew about his presence was the
sudden and shocking grasp of his hands on her re-
cumbent body as she lay asleep.

She woke immediately, crying out in fear and
bewilderment.

Luke shook her.

She stared at him, confused and disorientated.

'You're not wearing any clothes.' Her bemused
brain formed the words before she could silence
them, and then her eyes widened in shock as the
bedroom door opened and her grandmother walked
in.

'Luke, I heard someone call out——' she began
as she entered the room.

Sara felt the tension grip him as her grandmother stood staring at them. Sara saw her shocked expression, and realised sickly what her grandmother must be imagining.

'No, Gran... You...' But Luke was before her, pulling on his robe, his voice calm and even as he said quietly, 'Alice, I'm sorry. Sara and I should have told you. We want to get married...'

Sara couldn't believe what she was hearing. What on earth was Luke saying? Then she looked at her grandmother's face, and saw the joy reflected there.

'Oh, my dears! Oh, Sara, this is exactly what I wanted!'

'I'm sorry you had to find out like this.' How grim Luke sounded, and no wonder! 'But it's been a long week, Alice, and I've missed Sara very much indeed.'

'I'm not so old that I don't remember what it's like to be in love, Luke,' Sara heard her grandmother saying. 'I'll say goodnight to you both now. No doubt Sara will soon be returning to her own room,' she added, firmly and diplomatically.

She was gone before Sara could protest. Her breath seemed to have leaked away somewhere deep inside her chest. She stared at Luke in bewilderment, wondering if he could possibly have gone mad.

He was standing well away from her, and there was nothing lover-like at all in the way he was looking at her.

'Very clever,' he told her gratingly. 'Such a neat and effective trap. Old-fashioned, of course,' he said it almost musingly, 'but effective, none the less. Cressy warned me that you were on the look-out for a rich husband, but I never imagined...' He broke off and looked unkindly at her.

Sara was appalled. 'You can't *possibly* think I want to marry *you*!'

'Cut out the pretence, Sara, we both know the truth. Oh, I don't flatter myself that you have any personal interest in me. Any rich man would have done, but with me, of course, you have an advantage. You know I'd do anything in my power to stop Alice from being hurt, and she would be hurt, wouldn't she, if she thought her precious "innocent" granddaughter was indulging in a relationship with a man to whom she wasn't married?'

It was archaic, impossible! And yet, what he said was also true. Her grandmother *would* be hurt. Sara had seen that in those few agonising seconds before Luke had made his unexpected announcement.

'So you've trapped me very neatly, unless, of course, you want to go to Alice and tell her exactly what you *were* doing in my bed.'

Sara looked at him wildly and then trembled.

'No, I thought not. By the way, what would you have done if she hadn't happened along at precisely the right moment? A clever idea that, to scream so effectively—and loudly.'

'I didn't scream. I was frightened—you shocked me...'

'By getting into my own bed?'

'You've got it all wrong,' Sara told him desperately. 'I didn't come here to trap you into marrying me. Gran was... was ill this afternoon. She made me promise not to tell you, but I had to. I thought it would be best if I waited for you here, so she didn't guess. You're normally back from London around eleven,' she added indignantly. 'I was tired...'

'You're lying.' The flat way he said the words was like a blow in the face. 'Oh, I don't doubt Alice did have a black-out—very conveniently for you, but I know too much about you to be taken in, Sara. I suppose, once you discovered there was no money in the family, you decided that marriage to me was the next best thing.'

'No money?'

'Bar the odd few thousand, that's why...' He broke off, his mouth hard. 'This whole discussion is pointless. We're committed now, just as you intended we should be. You've got what you wanted, Sara, but be warned. I intend to make sure you pay for it in full measure—very full measure. Now, get out of my room.'

She was too stunned to argue. How could he think she had actually plotted to trap him into marrying her? It was ridiculous, farcical! Like something out of a Jane Austen novel, when a woman could be compromised simply by being seen unchaperoned in the company of an unmarried man.

She was tempted to go straight to her grandmother and tell her everything, and then she remembered that quivering look of delight Alice had given them both.

Her grandmother wanted this marriage, she acknowledged painfully. Knowing the precarious state of her health, how *could* she go to her and tell her the truth?

In her grandmother's day, young ladies were not found in men's bedrooms unless they were engaged at the very least, Sara acknowledged wryly.

If only she had spoken up and told her the truth immediately, everything could have been explained, but now it was too late. If she told her now, she was going to be so disappointed.

But marriage to Luke? Her body shook at the thought. He couldn't possibly intend to go through with it. He was just trying to frighten her, to force her into being the one to back out. Well, she wasn't going to. *He* was the one who had announced that they were getting married, and so *he* could be the one to explain to her grandmother that they weren't.

There was no sign of Luke at breakfast, and Sara allowed herself to hope that last night had all simply been part of a hideous nightmare.

This comfortable fiction was destroyed by her grandmother when Sara took in her breakfast tray. Her grandmother was sitting up in bed, her face radiant.

'Sara, my dear, I've been making plans. You'll be married here, of course. Luke insists on only having a very small affair. He's even threatened me

with being forced to stay in bed until the ceremony
if I don't behave myself.'

Sara swallowed, her determination to force Luke
to be the first to back down from their bogus engagement forgotten.

'Grandmother, about last night——'

'Sara, there's no need to say a word. Luke has
already spoken to me.' She sighed. 'When a man
as virile as Luke falls in love...' Her voice trailed
away, and Sara was aghast to find herself blushing
beneath her grandmother's benign smile.

Grandmother thought that Luke had been
overcome by desire for her. It was as plain as though
she had actually said the words.

'No, Gran, you...'

'Oh, I nearly forgot. Luke wants to see you in
his study. You know which room it is, don't you?'

She did. It was the one room in the house Anna
was forbidden to touch.

'I'd better go down and see him, then.'

She saw from her grandmother's frown that she
had expected a more enthusiastic response, and she
escaped before anything more could be said.

There was an instinctive urge to stop and knock
before entering the study; she subdued it, her head
held proudly as she opened the door and marched
in.

Luke was sitting behind the desk, frowning into
a computer terminal. It looked very similar to the
one she had trained on in her evening classes, and
she looked at it with interest. So that was how he
kept in touch with his businesses in Australia!

She waited while he jotted something down, going to stare out of the window on to the rose garden. The roses were the old-fashioned variety. They had been planted by one of her ancestors.

'Gran said you wanted to see me.'

'There are things we need to talk about.'

'Such as how we're going to break the news to Gran that we aren't getting married, you mean?'

There was a tense silence, and then suddenly he was at her side, wrenching her face round to his so that he could look into her eyes. His fingers bruised her too sensitive skin and she flinched trying to tug away.

'Just what are you threatening now?' he breathed dangerously. 'If you say one word, just one word to your grandmother suggesting that we aren't getting married . . .'

Sara's head spun, whether from the shock of what she was hearing, or from the pressure he was exerting on her blood vessels, she wasn't sure.

'You don't *want* to marry me!' she protested.

'You should have thought of that before,' he told her tightly. 'Oh, come on,' he added when he saw her white face, 'you knew what you were doing. You know how much Alice means to me. She's the closest thing I've ever had to any family, and there's no way I can let her think I've callously seduced her precious grandchild—and you know it.'

He had hated betraying even that much to her, Sara noted numbly. She swallowed hard against the odd lump of pain in her throat, wondering why she should feel this surge of pity for him.

'I could have explained,' she told him slowly. 'Gran would have understood.'

'What would you have told her?'

'The truth,' Sara told him quietly. 'That I was waiting to tell you about her passing out, and that I fell asleep.'

'Dressed in nothing more than a flimsy robe.'

Hot colour shot through her skin. So he *had* noticed that.

'Oh, come on, even Alice isn't that naïve.'

'But you don't *want* to marry me. You don't love me . . .'

'Love isn't necessarily a prerequisite of marriage,' he told her sneeringly. 'Surely you don't think I haven't noticed the signals your body's been giving mine. My bed's been empty for a very long time, and your body will fill it as adequately as anyone else's, I'm sure.'

Sara was horrified by his cynicism.

'You don't mean that . . . What about Cressy?'

'Are you asking me if I've been sleeping with her?' he asked, deliberately misinterpreting her shock. 'If so, the answer's "no".'

'You don't love her, then?'

She wasn't sure why she had to be so clear on this point, only that it was very, very important.

'Love!' he laughed harshly. 'Love died for me a very long time ago.'

When her cousin had died, Sara amended silently. Of course, that would account for some of his bitterness, for some of the austerity she so often glimpsed in him. Having already been married to the woman he loved, having known love and lost it, he was quite prepared to marry for a second time because he knew it was what her grandmother wanted.

In that moment, Sara knew that nothing she would say was going to change his mind. As though he had read hers, he told her softly. 'Don't get any foolish ideas into your head, will you? You and I are going to be married, and if I even suspect that you're thinking of running out on me, I'll keep you locked up until we're man and wife.'

Sara had no doubt that he meant every word he was saying. She looked at him with stunned green eyes, and knew with a sudden surge of sensation that the reason she was not objecting far more vociferously that there was no way she was going to marry him was because a tiny part of her wanted to.

It shocked her to her heart, cutting through all her previous self-knowledge. Where had it come from, this foolish romantic desire to teach this hard, unmovable man to believe in her, and more, to teach him to *love* her?

She shuddered with the enormity of it, knowing with every scrap of sanity she possessed that what she wanted was impossible; that if she had any sense she would fight with everything she possessed to make Luke change his mind about this marriage. But, instead of opening her mouth and telling him so, she simply stood there, almost transfixed, while he released her and strode back to his desk.

*   *   *

That evening he presented her with an engagement ring. She had no doubt that he had gone into Chester especially to get it, but what did surprise her was its perfect fit.

It was a flawless, antique emerald in a twisted gold setting, and she loved it immediately.

'Thank you,' she said shakily, resisting a fierce temptation to turn her head away as his lips touched hers.

It wasn't like that other kiss; this one was cool and clinical, and yet she still couldn't stop her mouth from trembling beneath his. She swayed slightly, freezing as she heard her grandmother's soft happy laugh.

'Don't overplay your part too much,' Luke advised her in a cool breath against her ear. 'The hunted virgin bit is taking it a little too far.'

She hated the cynical way he was looking at her, but it was too late now to protest her innocence.

She was dreading telling Cressy about what had happened but, as though fate had decided to relent, on the very next morning her stepsister rang to announce that she wouldn't be coming that weekend, nor for several weekends to come, as she had, after all, got an audition for the American soap.

'I shall stay over there for a few weeks. It will give Luke an opportunity to miss me.'

She rang off before Sara could pluck up the courage to tell her, and it was only later in the evening that she realised that Luke might want to break the news to Cressy himself.

Gran had taken to leaving them alone together in the evenings, and Sara dreaded this ordeal more and more each evening. It was always a relief when Luke stood up and announced that he had work to do, thus freeing her to either go to bed, or find some alternative way of passing the evening.

It struck her that already she was beginning to wilt under the silent war of nerves she and Luke seemed to be engaged on. He delighted in deliberately tormenting her, it seemed; his kisses in Gran's presence were always so studiedly tender and reverent, yet holding all the acid content of his dislike, making a mockery of all that she had always believed a relationship between a man and a woman should be.

What hurt most of all, though, was her own inability to stop her treacherous body from responding to his touch. It seemed he only had to look at her mouth and her whole nervous system went into overdrive.

It was useless telling herself that it was only desire; she knew herself too well for that.

Somehow or other, she had managed to fall in love with him. How was it possible to love a man she didn't like? A man who, moreover, despised and disliked her?

Luke claimed that she had caught him in a well-planned trap, but in reality she was equally trapped. Those kisses, those small, delicate intimate touches of his fingertips against her skin; they were all a deliberate torment. She knew that. Somehow he had recognised her physical responsiveness to him, and now he was playing on it, using it to hurt her.

She could only be thankful that he felt no corresponding physical desire for her. She didn't know how on earth she could ever have brought herself to endure his lovemaking, knowing it was only generated by physical desire.

They were married exactly three weeks after Gran had found them together in Luke's bedroom.

It was a small affair, with friends of Gran's and a few neighbours. Sara's aunt did not fly back from Australia, but no one had expected her to.

She would not want to see her daughter's husband marrying someone else, Sara suspected.

She wondered if Gran missed her son but, when she broached the subject, Alice Fitton shook her head.

'It is always the women who have loved Fitton Place best. It is always the women of this family who have cherished and kept it. I had thought your mother...'

They weren't having a honeymoon.

Gran had to go to London to see her specialist almost immediately after the wedding, and they were going with her.

No one seemed surprised that they were marrying, although Andrew had been openly disappointed. Sara had liked him, but that was all. She glanced now at the tall, dark-suited man at her side. She had decided against a traditional wedding dress, not wanting to remind Luke of his first wedding.

Instead, she was wearing a slightly twenties-style, cream lace two-piece, with a very simple, flower-trimmed hat.

The village church wasn't large. The sun was shining for them, and the village turned out in force. So why did this sense of unreality persist? Why was she having so much trouble in actually believing she was Mrs Luke Gallagher?

There seemed to be a frozen emptiness of space where her heart normally was, all normal emotion had been completely suspended from the moment she had entered the church. Now they were all back at the house, eating the delicious buffet Anna had prepared. Tom was hovering importantly at her side. He was almost as thrilled as Gran about the wedding.

'It's time for us to leave.'

Sara stared stupidly up at the man who was now her husband.

'It is the customary thing for brides and grooms to do...'

'But I thought we were staying here...'

'Not tonight,' Luke told her quietly. 'I've booked us into a local hotel. Don't say anything. You don't want your grandmother to think we're falling out already, do you?'

Sara glanced helplessly from his set face to her grandmother's caring one. Of course he was right, and she supposed she should have guessed that they would be expected to spend at least one night alone together, but she had been so bemused by everything...

The very last thing she wanted was this—to be alone with him, she admitted half an hour later, as his powerful Jaguar saloon pulled away from the house. The very last thing!

CHAPTER SIX

THE ROAD Luke took was unfamiliar to Sara, heading away from Chester and the Welsh hills rather than towards them, and slightly south.

Any normal bride at this juncture would surely be asking her new bridegroom where they were going, if she didn't already know.

For goodness' sake, stop acting like a mouse, she chided herself valiantly, after darting a timorous glance at Luke's unforthcoming profile.

She cleared her throat and tried to pretend he was merely an acquaintance with whom she was sharing a brief car ride, and to treat him accordingly.

They *were* married; there was nothing she could do about that. For her grandmother's sake, she had to find a way of living with that fact.

Strange, the tricks even the most logical of human brains could play on one. Up until now she had barely given a thought to the future. Her fears, her doubts—these had all centred round the threat Luke had made when he had warned her against trying to defy him.

Now that they were married, it was as though a befuddling fog had cleared from her mind, and she was left with an appalling mental picture of what her future life was going to be.

Luke was never going to believe that she had not deliberately inveigled him into marriage. The small, burgeoning tendrils of emotional response she had felt towards him; that frisson of excitement-cum-apprehension she experienced whenever he came close to her; that awareness of him as a man and her wholly female response to him; these would surely wither and fade in the arctic wasteland of his contempt for her.

Love needed time to grow, to mature; hers would not be given that time. Better, surely, to have stood firm, faced her grandmother with the truth and prayed that her disappointment did not have an adverse effect on her health, than to endure what was to be.

Luke turned the car into what could have been the drive to a private house, had it not been for the small, discreet brass plate set into one of the gateposts.

Butterflies exploded in her stomach. There was no point in wishing she could turn back the clock; this was now, and somehow it would have to be lived through.

She stole another quick glance at Luke's profile. He had not uttered one word to her since their journey had commenced. She wished she could borrow from him a little of his will-power, his ability to put aside his own feelings; then she could ignore his own contempt for her, and concentrate instead on her grandmother and the happiness their marriage would bring her.

She shivered as she recognised the strength of such a will-power and wondered, a little sadly, if Luke ever succumbed to the very human weakness of emotional self-indulgence. Even in his contempt for her, he was controlled, apart from that one occasion when he had kissed her.

Her eyelashes flickered rapidly, a frantic pulse beating in her throat.

She had nothing to fear, she reassured herself as he brought the Jaguar to a standstill. That had been a momentary aberration, a strong and very angry male's only release for the powerful rage generated in him by a weaker and female foe.

No, Luke would not kiss her again. So why did she feel this odd breathlessness, the jumpy, tense edginess?

She made to get out of the car, impressed by the ivy-clad stone exterior of the hotel.

The building looked Victorian and immaculately cared for, with smooth green velvet lawns stretching down to a small lake.

She reached for her door-handle, startled to see that Luke was already opening it for her. Even though he thoroughly despised her, his manners were impeccable. *Noblesse oblige,* she thought a little acidly, wondering how he would react if he ever came to realise how much he had misjudged her. She ought to find the prospect of his discovery very satisfying, but it was rather like indulging in the romantic daydream of pretending one was on one's way to a tropical island, when in reality one was sitting on the Underground on the way to work—a pleasant, but hardly realistic exercise.

A uniformed porter came out to take their cases. Who had packed hers, she wondered, and what with? Luke's hand under her arm made her feel like a prisoner being escorted to the guillotine. She subdued the hysterical bubble of laughter welling up inside her throat. Unlike her, Luke appeared perfectly calm and relaxed. But then, he had been through this before, she reminded herself bitterly, and hated herself for her cynicism.

Luke's first marriage to her cousin had been a love match. No doubt, even before they went on honeymoon, they would have been lovers.

She tried not to show her shock as her mind suddenly relayed to her a mental image of Luke's naked and aroused body. She shivered and closed her eyes, trying to dismiss the image, but it only came clearer.

'You're not running out on me now.'

The harshness of his voice brought her back to reality. The porter was too far away to have heard him, but Sara looked round instinctively.

'This way.' Luke's grip on her arm tightened, as though he suspected that she might actually try and make a run for it.

The thought of doing so made her grimace a little wanly. It was too late for running now.

A curious numbness overcame her, a sense of drugging recognition of the inevitability of her fate. So must many, many of her sex have felt through the ages, and this, no doubt, was why she herself was so susceptible to the sensation now. It was part of the feminine psyche, a primitive inheritance that carried with it the weight of the past.

Over the centuries, there must have been many women from her family who had been married to men against their will. Perhaps that was even why she had not objected more strenuously. Perhaps...

Her wild, disordered thoughts were scattered like doves in the face of an attacking hawk, as Luke directed her towards the stairs. He had signed in for them both she realised, her mind still dazed.

'This way,' he told her curtly.

The hotel foyer was comfortably furnished, in the manner of a rather luxurious country home.

The other guests were mainly middle-aged, elegantly dressed women and their husbands.

Through an open doorway, she caught a glimpse of the restaurant, leaded windows overlooking the gardens, tables set with crisp cloths and truly beautiful flowers.

The whole place had the ambiance of a privately owned country manor, she recognised as Luke directed her toward the stairs.

If there *was* a lift, it was tucked discreetly out of the way somewhere. As they went upstairs, there were no chattering maids about, no busy waiters; no evidence that the place was a hotel at all.

In other circumstances, she would have been thrilled by the luxury of the place, but right now...

Luke stopped outside one of the panelled doors and unlocked it.

They had a suite, Sara recognised, subduing a sense of awe as she walked into the beautifully furnished sitting-room.

Someone with both flair and money had planned this décor, this muted blending of blues and terracottas, to achieve such a harmonious and individual whole.

A fire burned in the open fireplace, and a log basket was filled with logs. A bucket of champagne and two glasses on a silver tray caught her eye.

The intimacy of the sitting-room, with its fire and its two chairs pulled up beside it, suffocated her. She wanted to run towards the door and pull it open; she wanted to deny that she and Luke had any reason for sharing these surroundings. Surroundings discreetly designed for lovers, she recognised now; whether of the well-married and comfortably established variety, or the new, slightly nervous kind.

The whole ambiance of the room was chosen to lap one in warmth and security, to provide a retreat from reality and the outside world.

Here one could pretend that no one else existed, that the world was excluded and that it could not break in.

What on earth had made Luke choose such a place? He must surely have known.

A discreet tap on the door signalled the arrival of their luggage. The porter carried their cases through into a room beyond the sitting-room.

A room... Her heart thumping, Sara waited until Luke had tipped him and he had gone, and then demanded baldly, 'How many bedrooms does this suite have?'

'One,' Luke responded imperturbably, plainly not the slightest bit disconcerted by her question.

'One, but... Why aren't we having separate rooms?'

'On our *honeymoon*?' One dark eyebrow lifted, his mouth curving in a smile of cynicism.

'But...'

'I told you the night you trapped me into this marriage that you would have to pay a price,' Luke reminded her grimly. 'Now is that time.'

And the price would be... Her eyes widened, and she backed away from him, her hand going protectively to her throat.

'You can't mean...' She looked wildly and betrayingly at the bedroom door and swallowed, unable to finish putting her fears into words. Luke couldn't mean that he intended that they should consummate their marriage, could he?

She looked at him, desperately seeking for some sign in his face that he was simply tormenting her, threatening her, but there was none. He meant what he had said.

'I'm not staying here,' she told him unevenly, picking up her bag. 'I'm leaving right this minute!'

'How?'

The calm disinterest in his voice stopped her.

'You don't have any means of transport, nor, I suspect, do you have much money—this hotel is ten miles from the nearest town, and closer to thirty from Alice's. And even if you did leave, where

could you go? Back to Alice? What would you tell
her? That the marriage was a mistake? After four
hours?'

Every word he said pushed home to her how
trapped she was. Every word was perfectly true.
Her handbag contained less than five pounds. She
had not even got her credit cards with her. Oh, he
had planned this so well! He had brought her here
deliberately, knowing exactly what her reaction
would be. If they were still at home... She
swallowed, desperate to prevent him from seeing
her fear. He would enjoy that, she acknowledged;
he would like knowing that she was afraid of him.

'You can't make me do this,' she told him quietly.
'If you... if you go through with this, it will be
rape.'

She looked defiantly at him as she said it. After
all, she was speaking no less than the truth. What
he was planning was rape. All right, so his pos-
session of her was legalised by the marriage vows
they had so recently exchanged. Vows that... Suddenly, tears stung her eyes as she called to mind the
exact words of the service: 'With my body I thee
worship...'

Only what he planned for her wasn't worship,
but punishment... a punishment of the most dam-
aging and cruel kind.

'Rape?' His eyebrow lifted again. 'Oh, I don't
think so.'

His calm sureness checked her. What did he
mean? If she wasn't willing to consummate the
marriage, then it must be rape.

'It *will* be rape,' she repeated huskily, as though, by saying the words, she would somehow banish the powerful effect he seemed to be having on her will-power. He was looking at her in such a way that suddenly nothing seemed to have any reality any more other than the dark glitter of his eyes. Her heart jumped nervously in her chest, a tension unlike anything she had experienced before seizing her.

She looked wildly into his face, and her breath caught in her throat.

A curious feeling that she had somehow walked out of reality and into some unfamiliar topsy-turvy sphere engulfed her.

'It will *not* be rape,' Luke repeated softly, and before she could divine his intentions he crossed the small distance that separated them and picked her up.

The immediacy of his determination held her in frozen thrall until they were in the bedroom, and then the sight of the hand-painted, half tester bed with its luxurious hangings shocked her out of her trance and she started to struggle, pummelling frantically at Luke's chest, knowing that there was no way she was going to be able to escape and yet driven relentlessly to waste her fragile strength in trying to defy him.

Evening sunlight gilded the room as Luke undressed her with humiliating ease. In the end she stopped fighting him and lay instead, still and cold, fixing her gaze on a point beyond him.

The other guests would be preparing for dinner, but they were honeymooners and no one would be so indiscreet as to disturb them; round and round went her thoughts spinning her out of control as she fought to deny the fear running through her.

Luke undressed. She could have got up then and escaped from him but to where and for how long?

He was right, she could not go back to her grandmother and tell her that the marriage was over almost before it had begun.

He had planned to inflict this—this humiliation on her all along. Perhaps that was even part of why he had married her. So that he would have the right to torment her as he chose.

Dark thoughts whirled chaotically through her mind, images she fought to deny torturing her. From a long time ago, she remembered a family friend's favourite maxim: 'What can't be cured must be endured.' But from where did one get the strength to endure? How could she endure the punishment Luke had in store for her?

That he intended to exact full payment for what he considered to be her crime against him, she no longer doubted.

The burgeoning love she had felt for him, the delicate, unexpected frisson of sexual desire, these had gone, to be replaced by a cold, hard lump of sick dread. It was enough to drive her from her cool, withdrawn sanctuary, to protest huskily, 'Luke, please don't do this...'

His response was to silence her plea with the hard pressure of his mouth.

She wanted to cry out with fear and denial, and then suddenly, as though he had heard that silent cry and was responding to it, his mouth softened, the hard grasp of his fingers turning to a caressing stroke, his mouth wickedly persuasive as it moved on hers.

A tiny trickle of response warmed her, a faint, unsuspected vein of sensuality recognising the skill of his touch and answering it.

The transition from aggression to seduction was so swift, so total, that she had no time to martial her defences against it; it was like being given the pain-killer after a shocking insight into the pain; the relief so tremendous that one did not question the advisability of taking the drug until it was too late.

Neither of them spoke; there seemed no need. She clung voluptuously to him as he held her against his body, letting her feel its fierce message of arousal.

How odd that she had ever feared this delirium of pleasure, she thought hazily as she moved instinctively to accommodate the heat and weight of him, her body quickening from anticipation to urgency.

Instinctively, she accommodated him, gasping sharply when she felt a brief flare of pain, so quick and sharp that it was dying away before she registered it.

She heard Luke cry out something, a tortured, driven sound that fixed her gaze on his face. Contorted in the rictus mask of unbearable pleasure, it

was oddly vulnerable; so vulnerable, that her throat
ached sharply with emotion. She wanted to gather
him to her and protect him from whatever it was
that tormented him, and then, dizzyingly, she was
caught up in the first climactic burst of her own
pleasure, stunned and awed by the immensity of it,
lost in the fevered storm that rose and fell within
her.

Luke cried out sharply, his eyes wide and blank,
his breathing harshly erratic. The intense desire had
weakened him more than it weakened her, Sara recognised, lost for a moment in the marvel of this
discovery, of knowing, however briefly, that she
held this powerful man in thrall. It was a moment
to be stored and savoured, as was the pleasure he
had given her, and the discovery that her fear had
been a child's fear, she recognised sleepily. And the
fact that she did, after all, love him. But now a
dazed lethargy possessed her, an unstoppable desire
to close her eyes and sleep.

As she did, she felt Luke move the comforting
warmth of his body away from her; she reached for
him instinctively, but she was already falling asleep.

CHAPTER SEVEN

SARA woke up sharply, as though someone had spoken right next to her ear, but she was in actual fact alone in the four-poster bed. Outside, it was daylight. She moved unguardedly, wincing at the unfamiliar areas of tension in her body.

Unwanted, worrying snatches of memory tormented her: words whispered and moaned in the blanketing darkness of the night, hands reaching urgently for her, and her own equally urgent response; a male body, a male voice, male hands and, worst of all, a name torn from that same male throat, as though drawn from a soul in torment. And that name had not been her own.

Soberly, she sat up, shivering in the realisation that she was naked. The pillow next to her own was smooth, but she knew that Luke had slept there.

How could she otherwise have had those elusive, haunting memories of him making love to her, not once but twice; and on neither occasion, as he had promised her, had it been rape. Far from it.

She shivered again, dismally admitting that Luke had known her weaknesses better than she had herself. He had not subdued her by force or coercion, but rather had used the needs of her own body against her.

From a purely physical point of view, she knew she ought to give thanks at having been granted such an accomplished and patient lover, but it was her emotions that tormented her this morning. Emotions she had thought had died beneath the cold cynicism of Luke's treatment of her, but which had surfaced last night, with a stronger, more dangerous depth.

When he had cried out his dead wife's name in her arms, it had been like being cut with a thousand sharp, aloe-tipped knives. Even this morning, the memory could still bring stinging tears of pain to the back of her throat.

He had loved her that second time with a fierce intensity, with a need that had shaken her to the very depths of her soul. She had looked into his naked face and had thought the need she had seen there had been for *her*—for *her* body, *her* flesh, *her* femininity—but she had barely been able to do more than take a small sip from the heady wine of power before the cup had been dashed from her lips.

Her love for him had welled up inside her, a generous gift from the victim to her foe. She had reached out to touch him, driven to find an unspoken way of conveying her feelings, and in that moment he had cried out her cousin's name.

She had known, of course, that he must have loved her, but he was such a contained, cynical man where she was concerned that, somehow, she had imagined that that love was now locked away in the past. She had never dreamed he would ever reveal himself or his pain so vulnerably to her; had never imagined that consummating their marriage would take him back to a time when the woman he had held in his arms had been a woman whom he loved.

She heard someone knock on the outer door of the suite, and hastily grabbed her robe from the bottom of the bed.

'Your breakfast, madam,' a slightly hesitant voice called out from the sitting-room.

Tying the wrap around her, Sara opened the door.

A young girl in a maid's uniform was standing beside the table she had just wheeled in.

From the silver coffee-pot came the aromatic scent of freshly brewed coffee. Golden-brown toast peeped from an immaculately starched napkin, a small disk of chunky marmalade stood beside fresh rolls of butter. There was cream and sugar, milk, fresh fruit and even a small, single portion of muesli beside a full glass of freshly squeezed orange juice.

Sara was bemused. She hadn't ordered any breakfast.

'Your husband said you wanted to have breakfast in your room,' the maid told her. 'If there's anything else you want . . .'

'No, no . . . that will be fine.' Sara smiled absently at her, and then rushed to get her bag to give her a tip.

The girl was obviously as unused to the luxury of the hotel as she was herself, Sara suspected, because she flushed deep pink when Sara gave her the coins.

Where was Luke? Implicit in his order for her breakfast was his own lack of desire to be with her. No doubt he had been more than pleased to let her sleep on. He was a proud man, her husband; and she had only come to recognise that rather late in the day. He wouldn't relish having betrayed himself to her so intimately.

She had challenged that pride, and he had punished her for it with his slow ravishment of her senses. Did he know exactly what he had done? How could he not? she acknowledged with wry self-awareness. Her body had responded to him too well, too thoroughly for him not to know that he had given her a pleasure she had never experienced before. He probably even knew that she had been a virgin.

Did he also know that she was dangerously, fatally in love with him?

She stopped her frantic pacing and walked over to the window. Several couples were strolling round the gardens. If this was a real honeymoon, if Luke shared her love . . .

Impatient with herself, she turned away. She would dress and then have her breakfast; there was no point in rushing to meet problems.

Sooner or later, she would have to face Luke. What would he do? Would he make any reference to last night? Would he . . .

She showered and dressed quickly. Her body was marked in several places with tell-tale bruises—not caused by pain, she acknowledged, her skin flushing a brilliant pink, but by pleasure. She even felt dif-

ferent physically, glowing with a deep-rooted sense
of completeness.

When she moved, her body had a feminine grace,
an assurance that, to her own eyes, was new. Would
others notice it? She was not naïve enough to imagine that all women felt like this the first time they
made love. She had been fortunate, and yet a part
of her would willingly have exchanged all of Luke's
skill, all of his finesse and ability to give her
pleasure, for the fumbling caresses of a man who
really loved her.

Maybe in time he would come to change his mind
about her, to... Warningly, the words of an old
proverb slid into her mind. 'Hope too long de-
ferred maketh the heart grow sick.'

Yes, she could see how that might be, how one
might wither and die, for ever thirsting after an impossible goal. She must not let that happen to her.

She had begun a new life now. She had new responsibility. Her grandmother, Tom and even, to
some lesser extent, Luke.

She had no idea how he envisaged their lives
would mesh. He was away a good deal, of course,
but when he was home... Would he expect them
to share a room? She was angry with herself for
the small jolt of pleasure that thought brought. No
wonder he had smiled so cynically when she had
thrown that accusation of rape at him.

She drank the orange juice and poured herself
some coffee. She was too wound up to eat. Where
was Luke?

Almost on cue, the sitting-room door opened and he walked in. He was dressed casually in impeccably cut sports clothes, every inch the English country gentleman, despite his Australian background. Why was it that tweeds could look so good on some men, and so disastrous on others? He was frowning, she noticed, subduing a shocking impulse to run across to him and embrace him. To hide the look in her eyes, she turned away from him, nibbling at a piece of toast she didn't want.

'We'll be leaving in half an hour.'

His announcement startled her. She dropped the toast and met the hardness of his eyes face on. A lump formed in her throat and she swallowed it, acknowledging painfully that there was going to be no acknowledgement of last night, no softening of his attitude towards her. What had she expected? Promises of undying love?

'I rang Alice this morning. Apparently, Tom has had an asthma attack. He's been asking for you...'

She started to shake. 'Why didn't you tell me this before? We must—I must get to him...'

'I've only just found out.' The flat, even tone calmed her. 'It isn't too serious. Apparently, he and Cressy had words.'

'Cressy?'

'She rang to speak to you apparently, and Alice told her that we were married.'

Without saying so, implicit in his words was their shared knowledge of exactly why Cressy might have found that news hard to believe.

'You...you didn't tell her, then?'

It was hard to speak through the pain in her throat. Guilt, awful and all-encompassing, had her in its grip. Tom was ill. Tom, whom she had sworn to care for and protect . . .

'There was no necessity.'

Why? Sara wondered. Because Cressy wasn't important to him, or because his relationship with her stepsister, whatever it was, would not be impeded by their marriage? Obviously, he had no idea that Cressy had intended to marry him herself.

'And I might ask the same question of you.'

'I tried to, but I couldn't reach her.' And she hadn't tried all that hard, either, relieved not to have to tell her stepsister.

Within half an hour they were on the road. Sara knew that Luke was driving as fast as safety allowed, but even so she was willing them to go faster, to get there sooner.

When they did, she hardly waited for the car to stop before yanking off her seat-belt and running into the house.

Alice met her in the hall.

'My dear, he's fine. A few days in bed, the doctor says——'

'So, the bridal couple return.'

Cressy was standing at the top of the stairs. To Sara's eyes, she had never looked more alluring, nor more dangerous. Sara wondered what on earth she had said to Tom, but she couldn't linger, not even to appease her stepsister, and so, ignoring her commanding pose, she rushed upstairs and past her, leaving her to wait for Luke.

Alice went with her, trying to reassure her as she opened the door to Tom's room.

The little boy was asleep, his skin waxen pale. As always after an attack, he seemed to have shrunk somehow. Or was it just that these attacks always brought home to her how vulnerable the human body was?

It was almost as terrifying to witness an asthma attack as it was to endure it. Over the years, she had forced herself to adopt a calmness she could not feel, and she was not surprised now to discover that her heart was racing at what felt like three times its normal rate.

'Sara, he's all right.'

The firmness in her grandmother's voice reached her.

'I promise you, it was only a very mild attack. I told Luke there was no need for him to bring you home. No need for him to tell you, really.'

She frowned, and as her tension relaxed Sara realised that her grandmother was telling the truth. Tom looked nowhere near as ill as he did after a severe attack.

It crossed her mind that Luke had told her deliberately, knowing that she would insist on coming home, knowing that their time alone together would necessarily be cut short. *Wanting* their time together to be cut short? It was a humiliating thought.

'Come downstairs and have a cup of tea. I feel so guilty about dragging you home. This should be a happy time for you... You've borne the burden of responsibility for Tom for too long, and now I

know you have the added burden of me. No, don't
deny it, we both know that I'm speaking the truth.
But you have a very strong shoulder to lean on in
Luke, Sara. I'm so glad you've found one another.
Both of you deserve to have happiness. Luke is
more like an son to me than a grandson-in-law. His
marriage...'

'Gran, I don't think we should talk about the
past.'

She didn't want to hear about Luke's relationship with her cousin; she didn't want to know how
much it had hurt him when he had lost her.

She let her grandmother persuade her to go
downstairs. Anna fussed over them both, insisting
that both of them were far too thin, and frowning
when Sara protested that she had barely digested
her breakfast.

There was no sign of Cressy—nor of Luke, and
jealousy, a sharp, searing knife of agony, turned
inside her.

She didn't know how long it was before Cressy
and Luke came back. She only knew that the pain
inside her was so great that she couldn't bring
herself to look at either of them. Instead, she chat-
tered aimlessly and breathlessly, filling the silence
that otherwise would have been tormented by the
deliberate way Luke was also avoiding looking at
her.

Now that they were back here, it seemed impossible that they could be married. The man who had
made love to her last night, the man who had skil-
fully drawn out the deeply buried feminine heart

of her didn't exist; he *couldn't* exist behind that cold, austere barrier of Luke's withdrawal from her, surely.

When she could stand it no more, she went upstairs, supposedly to check on Tom.

He was still asleep, but it was a relaxed, natural sleep. She went from his bedroom into her own and sat down on the bed. Could it really only have been this morning that she had viewed marriage to Luke if not with pleasure, then at least with equanimity? Where was that equanimity now? She was a bundle of too-tender nerve-endings, poised on the brink of a jealousy so deep and destructive that she drew back from it in horror.

'I want to talk to you.'

She jumped as Cressy walked into her bedroom and slammed the door behind her.

Her stepsister wasn't pretty now, she noticed with admirable, if forced, detachment. How mean those pale blue eyes could look when they were narrowed with malice the way they were at the moment.

'You think you've been very clever, don't you, getting Luke? It won't last, you know. He'll be bored with you within a month.' She laughed, the sound high and shrill. 'You're so stupid, Sara. Didn't you stop to question why a man like Luke would want to marry someone like you?'

Of course she would have, if she had not already known the answer. She turned her head away. How wearying Cressy could be when she was like this! In the past, she had always tried to humour and coax her stepsister out of these vicious rages, but

today, for some reason, she didn't have the energy—
nor the inclination.

'He married you because he didn't have any other
option,' Cressy told her tauntingly. 'I know that...'

'And so do I,' Sara told her coldly, standing up.
She marvelled at the levelness of her voice, when
all the time inside she felt so betrayed. Luke had
told Cressy *everything* ... Somehow, she had not
expected that of him, although she had no idea what
she thought he should have told her stepsister.

Cressy gaped at her.

'You *know*? And yet you still married him?'

Sara walked over to the window.

Neither of them saw the man standing within the
half-open door. 'Yes. You see, Cressy, I decided to
take a leaf out of your book.'

'You what?'

'I married Luke for his money,' Sara lied evenly,
amazed at the discovery of this hitherto unsuspected talent within herself.

'What did you expect me to say?' She laughed
brittlely, taking advantage of Cressy's shock. 'That
I'd fallen in love with him? Well, I haven't ...' She
swung round and came to an abrupt halt as she saw
Luke standing in the half-open doorway.

All the blood left her face as she saw the contempt in his eyes. She took a step towards him and
then stopped, pride coming to her rescue. What did
it matter if he *had* overhead her lie? He already
thought as badly of her as it was possible to think,
and yet deep down inside herself she ached to run
after him and to tell him the truth.

'Fool, fool!' she berated herself.

Cressy summoned her own forces and told her angrily. 'Well, you've got him, Sara, but you still have to hold on to him. I won't be in California for ever, and when I come back...'

'What did you say to Tom to upset him?'

Her abrupt volte-face threw her stepsister. Cressy stared at her. This was more like the familiar Sara she knew; so concerned for their young half-brother, only there was no emotion in her voice or in her eyes. No, this was a new Sara, a harder, colder Sara, who she was just beginning to realise could be a formidable enemy.

'Tom? I told him that Luke should have married me and not you,' Cressy told her, tossing her head defiantly. 'Honestly, such a fuss! You'd think you were his mother, not his half-sister...'

'Oh, Cressy, how could you? You know how vulnerable he is...'

'Because you've pampered him,' Cressy shot back. 'I'm beginning to think Pop was right. You molly-coddled Tom.'

Sara closed her eyes and was amazed to hear herself saying fiercely, 'Get out! Just get out...'

She had never, never spoken to her stepsister like that, no matter what the provocation. It had taken Luke to make her do so. Luke and her ridiculous, dangerous love for him.

Cressy didn't even bother to stay for lunch. Luke drove her to the station, while Sara went to sit with Tom, who was now awake.

'Sara, you and Luke are going to stay married, aren't you?' he demanded warily when he saw her.

'Of course we are.'

She crossed her fingers behind her back, praying superstitiously that she was right. If anything should happen to her grandmother, there would be no need for Luke to continue with their marriage, and in those circumstances... She shivered as though a cold wind had touched her skin, when in point of fact Tom's room was warm from the strength of the sun.

He wanted to get up, but she managed to persuade him that he must rest at least until tea time.

'Poor Sara, you're surrounded by invalids,' her grandmother commented when she went downstairs.

'Tom has every chance of growing out of these attacks... Perhaps I do tend to wrap him in cotton wool too much... What do you think?' she appealed to her grandmother.

'I think you're right to be cautious. Asthma is a very dangerous thing, and not unconnected with emotional trauma in some cases, I believe. Tom strikes me as a little boy who has not had the love and attention he should have received from his parents...'

Sara couldn't say anything. Loyalty prevented her.

'I'm afraid Cressy was rather upset by the news that you and Luke had married,' Alice Fitton continued. 'A very selfish young woman, that one. As

I have said before, she reminds me very much of Louise.'

Sara didn't want to hear about Luke's dead wife; she felt as though she had more than enough emotional burdens to bear already.

'You should be resting,' she scolded her grandmother, trying to change the subject.

'I'll tell you a secret, my dear. This heart of mine has been giving me problems for a very long time, but it's never let me down yet, and I don't intend to let it do so for a very long time to come. I'd like to hold my great-granddaughter in my arms, Sara. Another Fitton woman to love and cherish this house. Strange how history always credits the male line with such importance and magnificence, when it is, in fact, the female line that is always the strongest. Women are the more enduring sex, my dear. We are designed to endure, that is our great strength. Even in these modern times, we are the ones who nurture the new generation. A child of yours, whatever its sex, cannot help but love this house. I know that, but I find myself hoping that you and Luke will have daughters.'

Sara was too choked to be able to speak. What could she say? How could she destroy her grandmother's hopes by telling her that she and Luke were unlikely to have children? Unless... Unless she had already conceived his child.

Her skin burned at the thought, her body curiously light, her breath catching in her lungs. If only that might be so! Luke's child... Luke's daughter.

'Louise was to have borne Luke's child,' her grandmother continued, unintentionally shattering her dreams and making her face the reality of the fact that Luke could never want to have a child with her. 'But she...she lost it just before the accident.'

So Luke had not only lost the woman he loved, but their child as well. Strange how too much pain could have a numbing effect, as though one's senses could only endure so much.

Luke returned from dropping Cressy off at the station, looking very grim. He went straight upstairs, and half an hour later, when Sara went up to get changed, she heard him talking to Tom.

It was a shock to open her bedroom wardrobe and discover that her clothes were missing. She stood for several seconds, staring at the empty space, her brain too sluggish to understand where they had gone. Too much had happened to her in too short a space of time.

She felt almost punch-drunk on the after-effects of trying to absorb too much information.

'I asked Anna to move your things into my room.'

She spun round, her nerves on edge at the sound of Luke's cold voice.

'You expect me to share your room?'

'It is customary between man and wife. And we are most definitely that, aren't we?'

He was reminding her about last night, reinforcing his subjugation of her, and she felt the hot colour burn her skin.

'A masterly stroke, to retain your virginity so long, but it was wasted on me, I'm afraid. Even in these modern times, it is still a powerful bargaining counter, but you'll forgive me, I hope, if I say that I found your virginal state a little too contrived, too calculated. You're what—nearly twenty-four?'

She nodded, unable to speak for the pain erupting inside her.

'To have remained inviolate for so long bespeaks a very strong will, or a very low sex drive.' His voice was colder than Arctic ice as he added softly, 'And we both know it wasn't the latter, don't we? In the past, a bride gave her husband the gift of her virginity as a sign of purity, her intention to honour their marriage vows, as well as for more practical reasons, such as proof that she was not carrying another man's child—very important in the days when inheritance was often a vital issue. And a man cherished that gift and honoured the responsibility that went with it.

'Strange that, today, such a gift of purity should somehow be tarnished. Perhaps, like the ill-fated Anne Boleyn, your virginity was tainted by the use you made of it, to goad and torment the male sex. So, now you have your rich husband, my dear; be careful you don't find the price you have to pay for him is too high.'

Sick at heart, she watched him go, knowing there was no way she could ever bridge the chasm that yawned between them. His misjudgement of her was too deep, too all-consuming to allow for any frail bridge to extend between them.

At dinner, she kept up what pretence she could. Her grandmother remarked several times on her forthcoming trip to her specialist, and Sara divined that she was very nervous about it. Tom had been allowed to get up and eat with them, and he was the only member of the quartet who was behaving in anything like a normal fashion, Sara suspected.

It was over coffee that her grandmother dropped her bombshell. Tom was in the kitchen with Anna, and the three of them were alone.

'Luke,' she began, 'as you already know, it was my intention to will this house on my death to a charitable trust. However, since Sara has come into my life, I have been having second thoughts.' She looked at her granddaughter and smiled wryly.

'My dear, a house such as this demands a great deal. Simply to run it costs a very large amount of money. Had you not been married, I should have hesitated to burden you with it, but knowing how much both you and Luke would cherish it, I have decided to change my will and to leave it to you jointly.'

She held up her hand when Sara would have protested.

'I am not being morbid, but we all know that my specialist is more than likely to recommend an operation. Such operations are relatively commonplace these days, but one should never take life for granted, and so I am telling you both now what I intend to do. I am seeing my solicitor in the morning, so if either of you would prefer not to be burdened with the house...'

'Gran, you can't . . .'

Luke's hand on her arm stilled her impulsive speech.

'We'd love to accept your gift, Alice,' he said quietly. 'You're right in saying that we both love this house. It is the only place I have ever been able to think of as home.' His smile was bitter. 'All the more strange, perhaps, when one remembers how much Louise detested it.'

Sara froze at the mention of his first wife's name. She was still shocked by her grandmother's generosity. To hear that she and Luke would one day own Fitton Place . . . She and Luke . . . Suddenly it struck her that here was another tie that bound them together. Was that why her grandmother was doing this? Did she suspect that their marriage was not all that it should be?

Sara could read nothing in the serene face opposite her.

'Nothing either Sara or I could do could ever match such a gift.'

Sara heard her grandmother chuckle.

'That's where you're wrong, Luke. As I was only saying to Sara this afternoon, I am very much looking forward to holding my first great-granddaughter in my arms.'

Sara felt Luke looking at her, probing her mind, trying to read what was hidden there. Did he guess how much she ached to conceive his child? Did he know of the fierce need that had been born in her today to have at least that tiny part of him to love without the taint of deceit?

She got up unsteadily, saying that she wanted to look in on Tom.

As she had suspected he would be, the little boy was deeply asleep. He always slept like this after an attack. She smoothed his pillow and picked up the book he had been reading.

'Odd, how such a very scheming woman should be such a caring substitute mother.'

She didn't look round, her throat too tight with tension to allow her to move.

'I thought you believed I was more interested in Tom's money.'

The bitter words seemed to jump from her tongue. There was silence, and she thought at first that Luke had gone, and then she knew he was standing behind her. The intensity of her body's awareness of him made her shudder openly, but she still didn't turn round.

'About that great-granddaughter Alice wants,' he said harshly. 'No child of mine will ever be used as a hostage to fortune.'

He was telling her that he didn't want her to conceive his child.

Oh, God, how could she bear such emotional agony? He hated her so much, and she, in her innocence, had not realised.

It was too late to wish she could recall those impulsive words she had flung at Cressy. Even if she tried to tell him the truth, Luke would not believe it, and what difference would it make if he did? she asked herself drearily. He didn't love her, he never would love her, and she saw now that nothing less than his absolute love would do.

It was pride that made her stand stiffly and turn round, her eyes shielded from him by the thick fan of her lashes as she said quietly, 'I assure you that the very last thing I want is to have your child, Luke. And, certainly, I made Gran no promises about a future great-grandchild, if that's what you're thinking. The assumption that we would have children was hers.'

'No...no, I suppose you wouldn't want children, would you?'

He sounded so angry that she was mystified. He had just told her he wouldn't allow her to have his child, and now he was turning on her as though...almost as though he wanted a child, and *she* was refusing to have one.

'Your sort never do, do they? They never want to burden themselves with unwanted encumbrances. I should have remembered that.'

There was a withdrawn, brooding look in his eyes, and Sara felt as though part of him had forgotten she was even there.

At eleven o'clock, she went to bed. She wasn't entirely surprised when Luke announced that he had work to do.

She doubted that he would wake her in the darkness of the night tonight, take her in his arms and transform the dreary travesty of their marriage into something warm and alive.

And she was right.

CHAPTER EIGHT

IT WAS amazing, really, that two people could live in such intimacy and yet remain so unintimate.

Luke was always up and dressed before her in the morning, and, if Sara did occasionally open her eyes while he was still finishing dressing, she always closed them again, as determined to preserve the façade of uninterest she had built to protect herself as Luke was to remain aloof from her.

He seldom came to bed before the early hours, but whether that was genuinely because of pressure of work or whether he was simply avoiding being with her, she had no way of knowing.

What also amazed her was the human capacity for pretense. In public, although he didn't behave towards her with physical affection, Luke still managed to create an aura of intimacy that was enough to deceive both her grandmother and Tom.

Today was the day that her grandmother had her appointment with the specialist. Tom was not going with them. Anna was going to look after him and, since they were staying in London overnight, Luke was driving them down in his car.

They were booked into the Dorchester, which apparently was her grandmother's favourite London hotel.

'I used to meet your grandfather there during the war, whenever he managed to get leave.'

Her grandparents' marriage had been a happy one, Sara deduced, and she had been surprised to discover that it had in part been arranged by their families.

'Not so much arranged,' her grandmother had told her, 'as wished for. Girls married so much younger in those days, of course. I was only twenty, and your grandfather twenty-eight. He was in the Navy, and our two families had known one another for years. There was a remote connection between us.'

Before they set out, Sara offered to sit in the back, but her grandmother protested that she must sit in the front with Luke.

Was it her imagination, or was that faint blue tinge to her grandmother's skin actually increasing? If they had had a different relationship, she could have discussed her fears with Luke. The circumstances surrounding their marriage, the fact that he had a totally erroneous opinion of her, precluded even the most casual kind of friendship between them.

All her life, a part of her had longed for someone she could turn to, someone with whom she could share her thoughts and fears. In part, she had found that someone in her grandmother, but deep in her heart Sara longed to be able to turn to Luke and tell him how very frightened she was.

These days women did not marry so that their husbands could shoulder all their burdens, she told herself bracingly. Marriage was an equal partnership, with both partners giving succour to the other in equal measure. She had no desire at all to play the 'clinging vine'. No, it was just that she craved that very special intimacy that existed between two people who shared a deep and very genuine bond. Stronger than her physical desire for Luke, which was very strong indeed, was a need to have some sort of emotional bonding with him.

It had got to the stage where she froze every time her dead cousin's name was mentioned, so great was her envy of her. *She* had known Luke's love; *she* still possessed it.

A tape of her grandmother's favourite chamber music filled the car, precluding conversation. Because Luke had no desire to talk to her, or purely for Gran's pleasure?

She bit her lip, trying not to think about how humiliating it was to share a bed with a virile adult male and to have him repeatedly turn his back on her, leaving a vast gulf between them.

Once, she had woken up and found that he had turned towards her, his leg thrown across hers, their bodies within touching distance. She had cried then, self-pitying, weak tears for something she could never have, or so she had told herself in the morning.

The drive to London was uneventful. A liveried doorman took charge of the car, and they were ushered into the impressive foyer.

Sara, used to the rather flamboyant way her father had of dealing with such people as doormen and waiters, liked the calm pleasantness of Luke's manner.

In no time at all they were being shown upstairs to their suite. This one did have two bedrooms, but one of them was, of course, for her grandmother.

Sara went to help her get unpacked, guessing that she would be apprehensive about the coming appointment, and hoping that her company would help to keep the apprehension at bay. She said as much very quietly to Luke, adding that she would come and unpack their cases later.

He gave her a rather odd look, as though both surprised and puzzled by her instinctive thoughtfulness.

It wasn't her fault that she didn't fit into the mould Cressy had cast for her, she reflected rather wryly as she left him.

Her grandmother was nervous, very obviously so, and although Sara had no experience of illness personally, she knew how tense Tom always got on these occasions.

With Tom, she simply held him and cuddled him, talking or reading to him. With her grandmother, she tried to distract her in a different way, asking her more about the history of the house and the families who had lived in it.

The appointment wasn't until three in the afternoon, but none of them did justice to the lunch that they were served. They were eating in their suite, and Sara couldn't help reflecting how much her life-style had changed. She had lived in London for years and had never once set foot in such a luxurious hotel, but when someone one loved's health was at stake, luxury was of scant importance.

It was Luke who took over her role of keeping her grandmother calm once they got in the taxi to go to the specialist's rooms off Harley Street. There was such a caring, gentle side to him where her grandmother was concerned. Sara swallowed a lump in her throat, knowing that that tenderness would never be directed at her.

The specialist's waiting-room in the elegant Georgian terrace was well decorated and comfortable, but it still had that aura of waiting-rooms the world over; even the air seemed tainted with the hopes and fears of the people who had been here. Her pulse was jumping nervously, Sara knew, and there was a strained look tightening Luke's mouth.

The specialist saw her grandmother first. She was with him for nearly half an hour—a lifetime, during which Sara didn't speak and neither did Luke.

It was so sad that neither of them could share with the other their fear for a person whom they both loved. Luke out of dislike and contempt, and herself out of pride and fear. Once she voiced those fears, she was all too likely to break down completely. There was nothing she wanted more than the luxury of being held in Luke's arms and comforted by the physical reality of him.

At long last, the door opened and the specialist asked them to join him. He was a tall, spare man with far-sighted, faded blue eyes and a calmly reassuring manner.

He explained carefully and simply that the leaking heart-valve causing her grandmother's condition was deteriorating, and that surgery was going to be necessary.

Both of them must have registered their shock, because he was at great pains to reassure them that the operation was a relatively simple one.

'And the benefits are enormous,' he promised. 'Most patients are amazed by the results.' He turned to Sara's grandmother. 'You'll find you'll be able to do things you probably haven't been able to do for years. Physically, you'll be stronger and fitter than you've probably ever been in your life.'

'This operation...is it...is it very dangerous?' Sara asked huskily.

He paused for a moment, and then looked at her.

'Potentially, all operations are dangerous, but I promise you, if I didn't think there was every chance of success, I would not be recommending it...'

He meant it, Sara recognised.

'So when do you suggest...' Luke began voicing what was in all their minds.

'The sooner the better,' came the prompt reply. 'You have a very good private local hospital with an excellent surgeon. I propose to telephone him this afternoon. With any luck, he will be able to operate at the end of the week.'

'So soon...'

Sara was barely aware of the choke in her voice.

'I promise you, there really is nothing to worry about,' the specialist told them kindly. 'You know,' he added, looking at Sara's grandmother, 'you should have had this operation before now.'

'I know, and I've kept putting it off, but you see, now I've found Sara...' She reached out to touch her hand. 'And now that she and Luke are married...'

'Quite so,' agreed the specialist. 'Now, there are just one or two things to run through.'

Before they left, he unlocked a drugs cabinet and gave Luke a small phial of tablets.

'Just a mild tranquillizer,' he told them. 'I suggest you have one when you get back to your hotel, Mrs Fitton. It will help you to relax, but eat first. The hospital will probably contact you direct, but you should hear from my secretary tomorrow with a date for the operation.'

They went back out on the street before her grandmother had any opportunity to change her mind.

'He's right, you know,' she admitted when they were back in the hotel. Afternoon tea was being served in the Promenade Room, and Luke had insisted that they join the other guests to sample this genteel luxury.

'I should have had the operation before, but I'm such a coward. The mere thought of undergoing an operation...'

'You won't know a thing about it,' Luke promised her, 'and with these modern anaesthetics... well, I suspect you'll be back on your feet before you know it.'

Before they went back upstairs, Luke excused himself to go and have a word with the reception desk. When he came back, he was smiling.

'I've managed to get tickets for *Phantom of the Opera*,' he told them.

Sara knew how much her grandmother had longed to see this musical. She had read all the reviews when it had first opened, and Sara had often heard her say how much she would like to see it.

Now she demurred that, with Luke and Sara so newly married, they ought to go out and enjoy themselves without her, but Sara was quick to reassure her that the evening would not be enjoyable at all without her there to share the pleasure.

Again, she sensed that Luke was watching her, although he made no comment. That came later, when her grandmother was resting, prior to going out.

'So you *can* be thoughtful when you want to be, even if it was contrived.'

'I love my grandmother,' Sara told him, facing him squarely. 'And I quite genuinely meant what I said.'

'Oh, I don't doubt that. After all, it means you won't have to spend the evening alone with me, doesn't it?'

Sara blinked, not sure if she was hearing correctly. Surely the boot was very much on the other foot? But caution and—yes, pride too, kept her silent.

Now she knew why Luke had insisted on them packing evening clothes. Sara had brought the new

dress her grandmother had bought her. She had lost
a little bit of weight, and the fabric made her skin
look almost luminescent.

Luke had arranged that they would supper in
their suite after the musical.

It was a wise suggestion, Sara thought; dining
out would probably have been too much for her
grandmother, on top of everything else that had
happened that day.

This was the first time she had seen Luke in
evening clothes, and her breath caught slightly in
her throat as he walked into the sitting-room. She
had deliberately vacated their bedroom the moment
she was ready, in order to give him privacy to
shower and change.

She saw him stop and study her, and she tensed
uncertainly. Was there something wrong with her
dress—her make-up? She wasn't used to dressing
up like this.

'Such a picture of almost madonna-like innocence.' The harsh note in his voice stung her sensitive nerves. 'How elusive you can be at times! It's
very effective, but then, I suppose you're well aware
of that.'

How she hated the irony in his voice! She wanted
to protest that he was wrong, that she was not as
he thought her, but she had condemned herself with
her words. And, even if by some miracle he did
believe her, what would it achieve? It wouldn't
make him love her.

They went straight back to the hotel after the
show, with her grandmother still raving about it.

The mask worn by the phantom was so effective that even now Sara felt almost haunted by the tragedy of the story.

She had cried once during the show, too caught up in the emotions of the story to stop herself. Luke had given her a handkerchief, and she had read in his eyes a totally male amusement for her female weakness. Just for a second, their joint barriers had been down. He had moved towards her as though to comfort her, and then her grandmother had said something and the moment had been lost.

After the supper they were served in their suite, her grandmother followed the specialist's advice and took her tablets. Sara went in to see her and found her on the verge of sleep.

If she should lose her grandmother now... She bit her lips, her eyes clouded with her fear as she went back to the sitting-room.

Luke was poring over some papers. He worked very hard, too hard perhaps, filling the empty spaces in his life with his work. Spaces left empty by the death of the woman he loved, Sara reminded herself.

'Is she asleep?'

'Yes. Luke, this operation... Is it...'

'You really *are* concerned for her, aren't you?' He got up and came over to her, gripping her chin gently and turning her face into the light. 'You've been crying again.'

She blushed as awkwardly as a small child, her face going even hotter as his fingertips traced the line of her tears.

'I love her so much. I'm afraid of losing her.'
Her voice wobbled, and suddenly she didn't care
any more about her pride. She was so frightened
and alone. Her grandmother was the first and the
only person who genuinely loved her, and the
thought that she might lose that love...

'I know it's selfish of me...'

'To love someone?'

The dark eyebrows rose, and Sara shook her
head.

'No, to be so frightened of losing her.'

'Not selfish, but odd, given the fact that you
stand to inherit very generously under her will...'

'You think I care about *that*?' She withdrew from
him abruptly. 'You think that *money* is more important to me than love?' she demanded fiercely.

Abruptly, she realised what she had said. Her
whole body froze, and they stared at one another
like two antagonists.

Sara was the first one to break the spell of silence
that held them in thrall.

'I...I think I'll go to bed. It's been a long day
and...and I'm tired.'

She was shaking violently as she undressed and
then showered in the enormous and very comfortable bathroom. The bed was unfamiliar, and she
couldn't sleep. Tension made her head ache and her
muscles clench. She was so frightened, so very
frightened.

She was still awake when Luke came to bed, but
she closed her eyes and lay still, observing the unspoken code they had evolved.

She heard the shower running, and tried not to imagine the muscled nudity of his body. The ache that had been with her since the night they had made love flared up sharply, and she rolled over, burying her face in the pillow to stifle the small sound of anguish rising in her throat.

She felt the bed depress as Luke climbed in, and immediately her tension increased. He had turned off the lamp, and the room was in darkness. The double glazing muted the sound of the London traffic, but it was still there. Strange how it had not bothered her while she'd lived in the city, but now, after the quiet days of Fitton Place, she was immediately and irritatingly aware of it.

She turned over restlessly, longing to be able to sleep. There were more and more nights like this recently; nights when she would wake just after Luke came to bed and then lie there aching for him, longing to be able to reach out and touch him, needing him as a lover and as a friend.

She moved again, and then stiffened as she felt her leg muscles cramp. The pain that shot through her was agonising. So much so that she couldn't stop herself from crying out as she struggled to sit up and escape from the excruciating discomfort gripping her body.

'What is it?'

She could barely speak for the pain. 'Cramp...'

She could feel her skin dampening with sweat as she fought against the locked muscle, and then the warmth of Luke's hands slid over her, seeking and finding the bunched sinew.

The relief was exquisite, the pain fading slowly as he expertly massaged her leg, leaving only a dull ache.

In her agony, she had kicked aside the bed-clothes and, as the immediacy of her pain left her, she realised that Luke had exposed the whole length of her leg, from the thigh downwards. She quivered, unable to suppress the fierce shaft of desire surging through her. His hand still rested against her skin, and she ached for him to caress her, to love her.

There was enough light in the room for her to see the outline of his face. She expected him to move away immediately he realised the cramp had gone, but he didn't.

She looked at him, and heard herself saying words she had never dreamed she would say to any man, her voice liquid and soft with desire.

'Make love to me, Luke. Please make love to me tonight.'

He moved and she tensed herself for his with-drawal, her skin going hot with shame and shock, and then his hands were on her shoulders, dragging her against his body, his mouth hard and de-manding on her own.

It was a dream, it had to be; and yet the things she was feeling were real enough. They welled up inside her, making her cling eagerly to him.

'Beautiful. So beautiful.'

His voice was unfamiliarly slurred, drugged almost, the touch of his hands hungry and yet . . . and yet tender, she recognised through the jolts of pleasure running through her like liquid fire.

Luke took hold of her, pushing her away from him.

His face was flushed, his chest heaving as he struggled to breathe.

'Oh, God, what are you trying to do to me? I shouldn't want you. I try to tell myself that I *don't* want you, but the minute you touch me...'

He made a sound of anguished protest, and then reached blindly for her, slanting his mouth across hers and holding her still while he ravished it with fierce, biting kisses that gradually softened and deepened until her whole body was responding.

'I shouldn't be doing this.'

She heard the strangled words, and knew he shared her own sense of almost hurting immediacy. As though another woman had taken her over, discarding the shy, almost prim Sara she had always thought herself to be, she discovered she was touching him, caressing him. She cried out his name as pleasure spilled through her in a quick torrent that she knew was only a preliminary to what she would feel, driven to keep him with her by whatever means she could, her body responding instinctively to the needs of her love.

She fell asleep in Luke's arms, oblivious to the pain in his eyes as he watched her.

They returned to Cheshire in the morning. As he had promised she would, the specialist's secretary rang first thing to tell them that the operation was scheduled for the end of the week.

Seeing the fear cross her grandmother's face, Sara reflected that it was probably just as well that she wouldn't have a long wait.

Once they arrived home, Anna and Tom had to be told the news.

Tom had become very attached to her grandmother, and Sara had to suppress a small smile as he assured her gravely that hospital could be 'quite nice'.

'I've been in lots of times, haven't I, Sara?' he asked proudly.

'Well, not lots,' she amended, 'but certainly several.'

And so he had as a younger child, when his asthma attacks had been so frightening that their doctor had insisted on him being hospitalised.

'Yes, and you always stayed with me, didn't you, Sara?'

'*Sara* stayed with you?' Luke intervened, frowning, his eyes questioning Sara, although his words were for Tom.

'My father and Laura were often away on business,' she explained evenly. 'It seemed only sensible that I should look after Tom.'

She didn't want to go into any further detail in front of Tom. He was sensitive enough to know that his father especially had always semi-rejected him, but Luke wouldn't let the subject drop and said tersely, 'But I understood that *Cressy* looked after Tom.'

'Cressy?' Tom scowled. 'I know she's my sister, but sometimes I don't like her. Why does Luke think that Cressy looked after me, Sara?' He looked up at her, and Sara ruffled his hair.

'Oh, I think he must have misunderstood something that Cressy told him, Tom,' she explained levelly, looking at Luke.

'Yes, sometimes it is possible to make mistakes about people—to misinterpret things that are said,' Luke agreed, equally evenly, but the way he was looking at her told Sara that he was thinking about last night. Just the memory of the way she had clung to him and had begged for his lovemaking was enough to make her look away in embarrassed confusion.

She had tried not to think about last night—not to remember how ardently she had responded to Luke's touch, how much she had wanted him. She had asked him to make love to her and he had done so, but it had been his first wife he had thought of when he held her in his arms. Just hearing Tom's artless remarks about Cressy wasn't going to change his opinion of her. How could it? That had been formed before he had even met her or her stepsister.

She was glad that the necessity of finalising all the details for her grandmother's operation kept her busy for the rest of the day. It meant she had less time to dwell on the shaming events of last night, and on the emptiness of her future with Luke. If they had a future.

The house would hold them together legally— but emotionally, physically? These were bonds that could only be formed with mutual love and trust.

And Luke did not love her.

CHAPTER NINE

ALL the arrangements were made. Her grandmother would go into hospital late Thursday afternoon, and the operation would be performed on
Friday.

Luke had originally planned to fly out to
Australia on Monday, but he had delayed his flight
for a further fortnight—another sign of how much
he cared for her grandmother, Sara realised.
Although he didn't show it outwardly, she knew
that he was just as worried as she was about the
outcome of the operation. She was beginning to
learn to read him now, and she knew that the tight
hardness around his mouth could denote pain as
well as anger.

He was a man who was more used to hiding his
feelings than showing them, perhaps because of his
early upbringing. She knew only the bare bones of
the story of how he had been orphaned very young
and brought up in a series of institutions. So much
more, then, must he miss the woman he loved.
There had been so much loss and pain in his life,
it was perhaps not surprising that he should treat
people with suspicion. No doubt he had contrasted
her apparently callous disregard for the relationship with her grandparents with his own lack of

loving relatives, and this had increased his dislike of her.

She knew that she was looking for excuses to explain away his animosity because it mattered to her so much that she *should* find a rational explanation for it; and that it shouldn't be based purely and simply on an antipathy towards her as a person.

She had caught him watching her more and more recently, as though something about her puzzled him. She knew that her behaviour was not what he might have expected from the person he thought she was. It was not that she had deliberately set out to change his mind, it was just that a caring attitude towards others came so naturally to her, that it was part and parcel of her life.

The close rapport between Tom and herself was something she had always treasured, and she had seen Luke watching them with something closely approaching pain in his eyes whenever she hugged or kissed the little boy. It was a look of loss, and something else she couldn't define, and she wondered if he was mentally comparing his own sterile childhood with the love she lavished on Tom. If so, she could well understand his pain. She had experienced it herself at one time. There could be nothing more hurtful to a child than to know that it is not properly loved, because a child reacts purely to instinct and cannot analyse why the love of a parent should be withheld. A child sees that lack of love as a lack in itself, rather than in its parent, and that child grows up always under the cloud of knowing that it has not measured up to its parent's desired image of it.

Such knowledge can never be totally forgotten, as Sara knew to her own cost, and she had been determined, from the very first moment she saw her father's reaction to Tom's illness, that Tom would not grow up under that burden.

He had always been a physically responsive child and she had been equally loving toward him. She did not believe in the adage that to kiss and cuddle a boy destroyed his masculinity.

She wanted desperately to have Luke's child, although she knew that was impossible. Luke had warned her that he would never allow her to do so, and she had no intention of subjecting any child of her own to the agony of being unwanted.

On Wednesday night, she went upstairs to check on Tom and say goodnight to him.

Luke was already in his room. The two of them were talking. Luke was very gentle with the little boy, displaying a side of his nature that she suspected she would never know. He was equally tender with her grandmother, and it said much for him, Sara thought, that such a strong, inviolate man should willingly reveal this inner tenderness.

She started to open the door and then stopped as she saw that Luke was sitting on Tom's bed, the little boy curled into the crook of his arm.

Tears stung her eyes. She had not seen Luke displaying physical affection for Tom before, and the sight moved her almost unbearably. Tom was looking up at him with such trust and love. Without

knowing it, Tom was giving to Luke the trust he
had never been able to give his own father.

'But what if you and Sara have babies?' Sara
heard him asking anxiously. 'Will you still take me
fishing?'

'Sara and I won't be having any children, Tom,
but even if we did, I promise you I'd still take you
fishing...'

Quietly, Sara stepped back into the hallway.
Neither of them had seen her, and she wished now
she had not eavesdropped.

Luke had meant every word he said when he told
her that he would not allow her to have his child.
She had thought that slowly, imperceptibly almost,
the barriers between them were lowering, but now
she realised she had been living in a world of
fantasy, imbuing his actions, the odd looks he occasionally gave her, with a meaning they did not
possess.

She had thought that he was slowly recognising
that he had misjudged her; she had even allowed
herself to hope that, although he could never love
her, he might at least come to respect her, but now
she saw that she had been imagining things.

He had married her for her grandmother's sake,
and he would stay with her for the same reason.
So, he had made love to her a couple of times. She
forced herself to face the truth. Physical arousal
for a man did not have to be accompanied by love.
On the first occasion he had been determined to
teach her a lesson, and on the second... She
swallowed hard. She had ... she had begged him to

make love to her, and he had done so. Although he had never referred to it, she suspected that he regretted that brief lapse. No doubt, in his mind, his physical involvement with her, however slight, tainted and contaminated the love he had shared with his first wife.

When he came out of Tom's bedroom, she was still standing there. He stopped abruptly, obviously surprised to see her. He was frowning, she realised drearily. He always seemed to be frowning when he looked at her. No doubt wishing her a thousand miles away, and out of his life altogether.

'Is something wrong?'

'No.' Her denial was immediate and harsh, but to her surprise he didn't leave her; instead he took hold of her arm and gently pulled her out of earshot of Tom's bedroom.

'I know what a strain all this must be for you. I can't understand why you deliberately ignored all your grandparents' previous overtures to you, I must admit, but neither can I doubt the strength of your love for your grandmother now. That couldn't be faked. Sara, there's no shame in worrying about someone you love. The moment I mention Alice, you stiffen up and spit at me like an angry cat. What is it that frightens you so much?'

Her eyes, shadowed and vulnerable, gave her away, as her glance skittered away from his.

'You're frightened of *me*?'

'Is that so surprising?' she asked him honestly, managing to find her voice. 'You've made your contempt of me plain enough, Luke. Is it so odd that I shouldn't want to give you a further opportunity to condemn me?'

'For *loving* your grandmother?' His incredulity couldn't be faked. 'Sara...'

'Luke...telephone.'

Anna was standing at the bottom of the stairs. Luke hesitated, as though reluctant to let her go, and Sara resolved the situation by pulling away from him.

She was too vulnerable to him, she recognised bleakly, too much in love with him to be able to protect herself from him. One hard look from him and she was ready to dissolve with pain. One small smile and her whole day grew bright.

She went to bed early, but she couldn't sleep. She was still awake when Luke came to bed, and she lay there with her eyes closed, listening to the familiar sounds of his bedtime preparations. He always showered before coming to bed, and against her closed eyelids danced erotic images of him...too erotic for comfort, she acknowledged, turning on to her stomach and trying to suppress the hot quiver inside her.

He walked back into the bedroom and her stomach somersaulted as she saw that he was naked. Normally, he wore pyjama bottoms. Or had he simply worn them for her benefit, or rather to reinforce his rejection of any intimacy between them?

She couldn't draw her fascinated gaze away from his body. He was everything she had ever imagined a man could be, and then some more. She ached to reach out and touch him. Heat shimmered through her veins.

'What's the matter?'

He stopped beside the bed, looking down at her. She realised that she had been staring at him, and flushed hotly.

'Nothing.' Her voice quavered slightly.

He pulled back the covers, and she protested impulsively, 'Your pyjamas...'

'I don't like wearing them,' he told her coolly. 'And, besides, what's the point? You've seen all of me there is to see. And anyway...' he paused as he snapped off his bedside light and then slid down the bed '...when you curl up against me in your sleep, I prefer the feel of your skin against mine without any barriers.'

Sara swallowed, unable to believe her ears. When she curled up against him? Did she? And what did he mean about liking the feel of her skin against his?

'That being the case,' he added urbanely, reaching for her, 'I think we can dispense with this, don't you?'

She couldn't move as he stripped off her night-dress and pulled her into his arms.

'No, don't push me away, Sara,' he murmured against her mouth, teasing it with biting little kisses. 'I'm frightened, too. I love your grandmother, too. In London, you asked me to make love to you... Now it's my turn to ask you. I need someone to-night, Sara, so please don't deny me.'

'Someone.' He needed someone. She went cold inside, and he felt her withdrawal, and reacted immediately to it, releasing her and saying quietly, 'I see. I suppose I should have guessed. The leopard never does really change its spots, does it?'

'Luke, I...'

Her throat was thick with tears, raw with the salt taste of them. How could she tell him that it was being reduced to just a 'someone', the pain of not being wanted for herself that had turned her body to ice beneath his hands? She had no words to tell him without betraying the truth—that she loved him, and that it was as a woman who loved him that she wanted to give herself to him. Not just as a willing body, not just an implement via which he could expend his sexual hunger.

'Forget it,' he told her tersely, turning his back on her. 'It wasn't that important, anyway.'

Not to him, Sara acknowledged miserably, because she herself wasn't important to him.

Both of them went with her grandmother to the hospital and saw her comfortably installed in her private room.

She was to be given a sleeping pill that night, and the sister in charge explained that it would not really be advisable for them to see her until after the operation.

'When...when can we see her?' Sara asked, dry-mouthed, as she and Luke left the room.

'Well, the operation should be over by lunch time. You can ring then, and I suggest that you

don't come in to see her until the evening. By that
time, she should be feeling a little better. Until then,
she'll be too heavily under the influence of her drugs
to be aware that you're here, and older ladies, like
your grandmother, hate anyone seeing them at less
than their best, don't they?' she finished tactfully.

She was right, Sara acknowledged. Her grandmother always looked so pin-neat and elegant that
she wouldn't want them to see her with her hair
uncombed and lipstick off. Trivial though these details were, in view of the seriousness of her condition, they would still be important to her
grandmother, Sara recognised. She had agonised
over what nightgowns to take and what bedjackets,
and she had insisted on Anna packing her favourite
lilac-based toilet water.

They were on their way back, driving down a
narrow country road, when a cyclist suddenly shot
out of a drive right in front of them.

Luke braked sharply, scraping the wing of the
car against a wicked-looking thorn hedge, but the
child, shocked by the near accident, couldn't control
the bicycle and fell off in front of them.

Sara was out of the car first, with Luke immediately behind her. He bent down to lift up the child,
and Sara said abruptly, 'No, don't touch him. He
might have broken something.'

She touched his arms and legs experimentally,
watching in relief as the dazed look in his eyes gave
way to realisation of what had happened. He sat
up unaided, his face almost green.

'Are you all right?'

'I think so.'

His jeans were torn at the knee, and he was bleeding. Dirt from the road was embedded in the lacerated flesh.

'I've got a first-aid box in the car,' Luke announced, reading her mind. 'Can you...'

'It's only a scratch. We'll soon have it cleaned up.' Her reassurance was more for the child than Luke, but to her surprise a look of gratitude darkened his eyes as he turned to go back to the car.

The first-aid box was well stocked, and in no time at all Sara had cut the jeans away from the wound and cleaned it up. As she had suspected, although it had been bleeding copiously, it was not very deep. The boy winced as she applied the antiseptic, but Sara had had enough dealings with small boys and bruised knees to know that the pain was not serious. Tom, for all his delicate health, was as mischievous and accident-prone as any other child, and she had never molly-coddled him, no matter what Cressy and her father had said.

'Do you live locally?' she asked him matter-of-factly, when she had checked gently once again for any major breaks.

'Yes. Here,' he told them, jerking his head in the direction of the drive he had emerged from.

'Luke, could you pick him up?' Sara asked without looking at her husband. 'He hasn't broken anything, but the shock... I'll take his bike, and go on ahead to warn his mother. If you arrive carrying him, she's bound to think the worst.'

'I don't have a mother. My parents are divorced.'

The truculent statement was underlined with a certain defensive defiance that Sara recognised instantly. Children suffered so much from the breakup of their parents' marriages, and were so sensitive about it. Many, many of them blamed themselves; their guilt intensified by their inability to truly understand adult emotions.

'Is there someone at home to look after you?' Sara asked him, frowning slightly.

'Not at the moment. We have a housekeeper, but she's away on holiday, and Dad had to go and see my gran. She's not very well. He won't be back until later.'

Impulsively, Sara turned to Luke. 'I think we should take him home with us. We could leave a note for his father. He's all right, but he could be shocked . . .' Although she didn't want to say it, her heart was touched by the angry defiance she sensed in the boy. He had pride, she recognised, but he badly needed someone to take care of him right now, and the natural vein of empathy for anything hurt and vulnerable that was so much part of her character would not allow her to leave him on his own in an empty house.

Luke was frowning, and she felt sure he was going to refuse. When he spoke, his voice was so clipped that she knew he was furious, but all he said was, 'Very well. There's some paper in the car. You write the note. I'll settle him on the back seat.'

It didn't take long. The car, despite a few ugly scratches, had nothing fundamentally wrong with it. The bike was stowed away safely in an outhouse, and they were back on the road within ten minutes.

As Luke drove, Sara questioned their passenger gently, but learned little more than his name. Instinct made her respect his need for privacy, and so she allowed him his silence and talked instead to Luke, filling the silence with gentle conversation that demanded little other than the occasional response.

Tom was openly delighted to have the companionship of another boy, no matter how briefly. They were very much of an age, although Ian was taller and heavier, and it made Sara realise how much her brother's asthma was already holding him back. She only hoped that the specialists were right when they predicted that he could grow out of it.

It was Anna's night off, so Sara made supper. Luke came into the kitchen while she was preparing it.

'I'm sorry about landing you with Ian,' she apologised uncomfortably. 'I realise you didn't want to bring him back with us, but we couldn't have left him alone in that house.'

'What makes you think I didn't want to bring him back?' Luke asked her quietly.

She looked at him. 'Well, you were frowning... In fact, you looked furious.'

'Furious?' He laughed, a harsh, odd sound. 'My God, jealous, more like. Is that what you really think, that I was *angry*?'

He shook his head and then walked out of the kitchen, leaving her staring after him in bewilderment.

Ian's father arrived half-way through the evening, full of apologies and concern. His thanks to her were almost too effusive, and Sara felt slightly embarrassed. She had done nothing out of the ordinary, after all, and she noticed that Luke was frowning again and, more, that he seemed to almost actively dislike Ian's father, who, apart from his effusiveness, was a very pleasant-looking man in his mid-thirties, with fair hair and a rather nice smile.

'We mustn't lose touch,' he announced just before he left. 'The boys seem to get on so well that . . .'

'My wife already has enough to do without adopting any more strays,' Luke interrupted brutally.

Sara stared at him, thankful that neither Tom nor Ian were close enough to overhear his words. Alan Jessop looked embarrassed, as well he might, and left them in some disorder.

Sara waited until they were alone before she turned on Luke and demanded angrily, 'What on earth did you say that for? The poor man was so embarrassed.'

'I was just letting him know that there wasn't any point in looking in your direction for a foster mother for his son,' Luke told her curtly. 'God,' he added savagely, 'what is it about you? Do you want to mother the whole of creation, is that it?'

He made it almost sound like a crime.

'I felt sorry for him,' she explained uncomfortably.

'Who?' Luke shot back. 'The boy or his father?'

'Ian, of course,' Sara said, shocked.

'Because he has no mother? Do you feel sorry for me, then? I had no mother nor a father,' he told her succinctly. 'Does that make you want to take *me* in your arms and cradle *me* against your breast? Well, does it?'

Sara didn't know what had got into him.

'You're a man, not a child,' she told him indignantly.

'Oh, yes, of course! And a man doesn't need the comfort of a woman's arms, is that it?'

He left her before she could retaliate, and she told herself it was just his anxiety over her grandmother that was making him react so violently. They were both on edge, both tense and frightened. She had been feeling queasy all day; for a couple of days in fact, and she knew that her nausea must be caused by nerves over her grandmother's operation.

Neither of them slept. Lying tense and awake through the darkness, Sara was equally conscious of Luke's inability to sleep.

In a normal marriage, a happy marriage, they could have found comfort in one another's arms. She shuddered slightly, aching to turn to Luke and burrow against him, but knowing that that solace was denied her.

By mid-morning the tension was a living thing, filling every room in the house. Even Tom was affected by it, asking anxiously every few minutes how soon the operation would be over.

The telephone rang just after eleven. Sara raced towards it, but Luke got there first. He frowned as he listened to whoever was on the other end, and Sara felt her heart plummet downwards. Unthinkingly, she clasped her hands together in an attitude of prayer. 'Yes. Well, thanks for ringing.' Luke replaced the receiver and turned to face her. 'That was Alan Jessop ringing to thank us for helping Ian.'

Her relief caused a physical reaction that had Sara rushing upstairs to the bathroom.

These bouts with nausea were beginning to drain her, and she knew without looking at her pinched face that she was losing weight.

They rang the hospital as soon as they dared, and to Sara's relief they learned that the operation was successfully over and that her grandmother was now in recovery.

Anna cried openly when they gave her the news. Sara wished she, too, could find relief in tears, but her fear had been so great that her mind still could not accept that the danger was well and truly past.

They left for the hospital later in the afternoon. Sara hadn't eaten all day, and she was feeling shaky and sick. An odd dizzy feeling came over her as she hurried out to the car, and she would have fallen if Luke hadn't seen her stumble and grabbed hold of her.

Held against the protection of his chest, she couldn't stop herself from sagging weakly against him. It felt so good to lean on him like this, to draw strength from his body and from the physical contact with him.

'Sara.' His voice was slightly rough. As she looked up at him, his fingers touched her hair almost gently, pushing it away from her face, as though he wanted to see her as he spoke.

'I don't know why you ignored all your grand-parents' pleas for you to get in touch with them. I thought it was because you were so damn selfish that you didn't give a damn about them, but I've seen you with Alice. I know how much you love her. I've seen you with Tom...even with that wretched child we picked up out of the road, dammit,' he added grimly. 'As soon as Alice is well enough to hear it, I think we should tell her the truth about our marriage. I thought...well, never mind what I thought,' he said harshly.

'You married me to punish me, didn't you?' Sara asked huskily.

'Yes.' His unequivocal acceptance of her accusation destroyed the last remnant of her hope that somehow she might be wrong; that somehow, during the brief weeks of their marriage, she had come to mean something to him.

'I set myself up as your judge and jury, and I convicted you because...'

'Because you thought I didn't care about Gran, and because Cressy lied to you,' Sara supplied emotionlessly for him.

Explanations weren't important any more. Nothing was important since he had told her that their marriage was over.

'I'm afraid we have to continue as we are until Alice is well enough to hear the truth. I'll renounce any claim I might have on the house. It should be yours, and I'll make that clear to her.'

'She'll be so hurt.'

His mouth compressed, and the way he was looking at her made Sara colour painfully. How odd it was that of all the conversations she had envisaged taking place between them, this had never been one of them.

She had wondered occasionally, when she saw him studying her, if he was beginning to doubt his original assessment of her. More than wondered, she admitted bleakly, as she stepped away from him and got into the car. Foolishly, she had actually hoped that he was. But of course, then she had never dreamed that his acknowledgement of his misjudgement of her would lead to him taking such drastic action.

To put an end to their marriage.

He got into the car beside her, and she couldn't bear to look at him, terrified that if she did so she would lose control completely.

'You were meant for marriage and motherhood, Sara.'

His quiet statement caught her off guard. She turned to look at him, and could make no response when she saw the bleakness in his eyes.

'But not with me.'

She shuddered as he set the car in motion. So now she knew, she thought numbly. Had he guessed that she had fallen in love with him, or was it simply that, having married her, he was now discovering that he couldn't live with the parody of their marriage, having already been married to the woman he loved? She must be a constant reminder to him of all that he had lost: his wife, his child. Sara blinked away her tears. She wasn't going to plead with him, and perhaps this was, after all, the sensible solution; the cut clean and sharp rather than a lingering, festering pain of being married to him and yet knowing that he could never love her.

'Christ, I should have learned by now, surely, not to try to play God!'

Sara winced beneath the harshly self-critical exclamation. She wanted to reach out to him, but she knew that her touch would not be welcomed.

It seemed to take for ever to get to the hospital. As the sister had predicted, her grandmother was conscious, although extremely drowsy.

She greeted them both with a smile, and Sara was astounded to see how well she looked, her skin pink and healthy.

They didn't stay long, and on their way out they were stopped by the surgeon who had performed the operation. When Sara commented on how remarkably well her grandmother looked, he smiled at her.

'Yes, it's quite amazing, isn't it? The body has tremendous recuperative powers, and your grand-mother is a very strong woman.'

'How long before she's allowed home?' Luke interrupted tersely. What he meant was, how long before he could end their marriage? Sara acknowledged.

'Well, that depends on her progress, but it shouldn't be very long. She'll have to take things easy for some time to come, of course.'

In the event, she was home with them within a very short space of time indeed, chastising Luke for wanting to employ a full-time nurse for her, and surprising Sara with her energy and vigour.

Three days after she returned home, Luke announced that he had to leave for Australia on business.

An excuse to get away from *her*? Sara wondered, absorbing the pain the thought brought and using all her self-control to smile calmly at the news.

Only that morning she had received a letter from Cressy, announcing that she had landed the much-coveted soap part and that she would be staying in California indefinitely. Sara felt sad about the relief her stepsister's letter brought. She and Cressy had never been close, but they *were* stepsisters, and surely with a little charity and give and take from both of them, they could have found some middle road, if only for Tom's sake? It was noticeable that never once in her letter did Cressy refer to her half-brother.

Luke was leaving first thing in the morning. She had offered to pack for him, and her offer had been brusquely rejected. It was almost as though, having made the decision to end their marriage, he now could not bear her anywhere near him. They still shared the same bedroom, but Luke came later and later to bed, and for the last two evenings she had lain awake beside him, her body stiff with loneliness and pain. There must be no greater gulf than that which yawned between two people who shared a double bed and yet remained on opposite sides of it.

The sickness which had dogged her since her grandmother's operation persisted. It worried her slightly, because she had never been a person who was particularly nauseous, but she put it down to the fact that she had never before experienced the emotional turmoil she was enduring now.

She also felt extremely tired. So much so that, even knowing that Luke would be gone before she got up in the morning, she could still not stop herself from going up to bed at just gone nine.

In their bedroom, his cases were packed and closed, a mournful reminder of the end of their marriage.

He had told her that he had misjudged her, but it had brought her no pleasure. It hadn't brought her anything, Sara thought miserably—at least, not anything other than pain.

CHAPTER TEN

SARA must have been asleep when Luke came to bed, because the first awareness she had of him was the whisky scent of his breath as he bent over her.

She opened her eyes and stared at him.

'Sara . . .'

He wasn't drunk, his movements were too steady for that, but he wasn't completely sober, either.

'Luke, what is it? What do you want?' she asked him sleepily.

'This . . . Just this . . .'

And then she was in his arms, with his mouth on hers, and he was kissing her with a wild hunger that pushed aside any thought of resisting him.

She could feel the fierce thud of his heart as it slammed into her. His body shuddered as he pushed her back against the pillows, his fingers tugging on the straps of her nightgown to reveal the perfection of her breasts.

He groaned as he touched them, caressing their tight peaks with fingers that trembled. She felt his mouth against her throat, hot and open as it slid over her skin, and she knew instinctively that he was going completely out of control.

The knowledge should have sobered her, but instead it gave her a wild sense of excitement, a feeling that this one time in his arms she could release all her own inhibitions.

She moved and, as though he thought she was trying to escape from him, he held on to her, baring her breasts to his gaze as he lifted away from her.

'No... Let me look at you.'

He captured her hands as she tried to cover herself, gently forcing them back on to the pillow either side of her head.

'Oh God, Sara...'

His hand actually trembled as he released her wrist to caress her rounded flesh.

'Sweet Sara, so generous... so tender. You even feel and taste tender, too, do you know that?' he demanded thickly.

And then he bent his head and kissed her with such sweet savagery that Sara felt as though he was drawing her heart itself out of her body.

It was an intimacy she had never expected to share with him, an intimacy that went beyond the physical joining of their bodies, because it was an intimacy that revealed, for the first time, a vulnerability in him, a need that he openly invited and begged her to appease.

It made her feel more powerful, more strong, more womanly than she had ever felt in her life. It brought to the final explosion of their rapturous bodies an intensity and meaning that held her wrapped in dazed disbelief long after the act of love itself was over.

And he stayed pillowed within the circle of her arms, his head resting against her breasts. Too sleepy to question his motives in coming to her, in wanting her so, so almost despairingly, Sara simply gave thanks for the unique gift his lovemaking had brought.

And yet, somehow, when she woke up in the morning and found that he had gone, she was not surprised.

There was a note beside the bed, on top of her carefully folded nightgown. She opened and read the contents. It said quite simply, 'Forgive me.'

Forgive him for what? For marrying her, for misjudging her, for making love to her? Yes, she could forgive him all those things, but what she could not do was forgive herself for falling in love with him.

It was hard to get up as normal and pretend that nothing had happened. She knew that last night had been the last night they would spend together. She even suspected that Luke might actually institute divorce proceedings while he was in Australia.

Her grandmother, who could be so astute, must not be worried or upset, and Sara was glad that another bout of sickness, even before she got downstairs for breakfast, gave her a genuine excuse for the pallid colour of her skin.

Alice Fitton eyed her granddaughter thoughtfully, wondering if Sara herself was aware of how much she had changed.

There was a new strength of purpose about her, a self-assurance that showed in the way she held her head and moved. And yet she was not happy.

Alice frowned and motioned to Sara to sit down beside her.

'I know something's wrong,' she said without preamble. 'What is it? Is it the baby?'

Sara's shocked eyes met hers. 'The baby? What baby?'

'My dear, you've been so sick, and tired... I...well, I naturally assumed that you and Luke... I thought perhaps you weren't happy to have conceived a child so quickly. Most newly married couples want to have some time to themselves before they start a family, and what with Tom and myself, you and Luke had barely any real privacy at all.'

'I...' I'm not pregnant, she had been about to say, but suddenly she wasn't so sure. A sick feeling of realisation swept over her. She *could* be pregnant—all too easily—and then into her mind slid Luke's words about never allowing her to have his child, and fresh panic set in. Luke was going to divorce her... If he knew she was having his child, he might try to persuade her to have a termination, give up her baby. Instinctively, her hand went to her stomach, the stomach she wasn't even sure yet did conceal a growing embryo, and she knew then, in that second, that there was nothing on earth that would make her part with her child. Nothing and no one.

She took a steadying breath and marshalled a smile, her brain working frantically.

'It's true, I might be pregnant,' she agreed, 'and you're right... Luke and I had hoped for a little more time together. I was going to make an appointment with the doctor this week.'

'I think you should,' Alice told her gently. 'You're looking very peaky, and it isn't wise to take any chances.'

She was thinking of her mother, Sara recognised. And she knew she couldn't add to the burden of her grandmother's worries by telling her that her child was very unlikely ever to know its father.

'Luke must be so pleased,' Alice Fitton told her gently, almost in fact, as though she had known what was in her mind, Sara thought wryly. 'Having lost one child...'

'This baby will never replace the child he would have had with Louise,' Sara told her quietly. 'I...'

She wasn't allowed to go any further, her grandmother looked quite shocked.

'Oh, my dear, I wasn't suggesting that! No, yours and Luke's marriage is very different to his first marriage, and as for Louise's child...' Sara didn't want to hear about Luke's first marriage. It hurt far too much.

'I must go,' she fibbed. 'I promised to help Anna...'

Luke hadn't said how long he would be gone, other than that it would be a matter of weeks, but he telephoned every night to check on her grandmother's progress, and Sara was obliged to talk to him.

It was a bitter-sweet experience, hearing the cool remoteness of his voice over the telephone and contrasting it with the husky passionate endearments he had whispered against her skin the night before he had left.

Sara lost weight. She felt listless and tired, and it was a constant effort to hide from her grandmother the fact that she was not blooming with love and happiness.

She had been to see the doctor and had her pregnancy confirmed. She must have conceived the first time they had made love, and her doctor had told her to expect an early spring baby. So far, only her grandmother knew, and she thought that Sara had already announced the fact of Luke's impending fatherhood to him before he left.

'Sara, you must try to eat a little more,' she expostulated one lunch time when Sara pushed away a barely touched plateful of food. 'When Luke comes home, he's going to think we've been beating you. Darling, you're so thin and pale... I know it's hard to eat when you're feeling so poorly, but you must.'

For the baby's sake, she meant, Sara acknowledged. Never once since she had first known she was pregnant had she even considered not going through with the pregnancy, and to hear her grandmother warning her, however gently, that she might be endangering her child brought weak tears to her eyes.

She ached for Luke. She lay awake at night, trying desperately to recapture those last hours with him, when the intensity of his passion had for the first time allowed them to meet as true equals. And yet, at the same time, she dreaded his return.

Wild schemes of simply leaving, of finding herself a job and accommodation in London, tormented her as the days dragged by. She couldn't bear to see his face when he realised that she was carrying his child. They should be divorced before it was born, but Luke would feel *responsible*. He was that sort of man.

And what of their baby, growing up without its father?

It was all such a mess, and with no way out.

The thing she dreaded most was a horrid suspicion growing at the back of her mind that, once Luke knew about the child, he would not divorce her, but would stay with her out of a sense of duty and respect. She didn't want that. It had been hard enough before, but how much harder it would be now if he were to stay with her after already telling her that their marriage was over!

He was very much a man, and there would be times when sheer sexual need would make him turn to her. Gradually, he must realise how she felt about him, and with that knowledge was bound to come contempt for her.

And what of their child? How would he or she grow up in such a traumatic background?

No matter how much she thought, how much she counselled herself, there was no easy way out, and in the end her final desperate option of running away was cancelled when Luke returned unexpectedly one hot September afternoon.

She was in the garden, weeding, while Alice had her nap. She had heard a car, but had assumed that it was Anna leaving for her afternoon off, until she turned round and saw Luke standing watching her.

She stood up awkwardly, all the blood leaving her face, her body swaying as she was caught up in the shock of seeing him.

She felt his arms reach for her and clung desperately to his strength. When her dizziness cleared, she saw that he was looking tired and thinner... much thinner. He released her bleakly, and motioned to the flowerbed.

'I thought Alice employed a gardener to do that.'

'She does, but I enjoy it. She'll be pleased to see you...'

His mouth twisted, as though something she had said had left a sour taste in his mouth. He was wearing a dark suit with the shirt undone at the top, and she was overwhelmed with a terrible need to reach out and touch him.

To stop herself, she rushed into hasty speech, 'You're back sooner than we thought. Did...did you manage to get through everything you needed to do?'

In her mind was the knowledge that, so far, she had received nothing to signal that he had started proceedings for their divorce.

'Yes. I've sold off my remaining Australian holdings. From now on, most of my work will be based in this country.'

Sara stared at him, almost missing a step. This was the last thing she had expected to hear. She had felt so sure that his first words to her would have been on the subject of their divorce, and yet it seemed as though it was the furthest thing from his mind.

No doubt because, as far as he was concerned, it was just a formality, she decided bitterly. In his mind, their marriage was already over.

'Is something wrong?' His eyebrow lifted as she touched her stomach protectively, an instinctive gesture she hadn't realised she had made until she saw him looking at her.

Angrily, she snapped, 'I should have thought you'd have wanted to retain all your connections with Australia.'

'Why?'

'Because of your wife.'

There was a pause and then he said quietly, '*You* are my wife, Sara.'

Was that really a questioning, almost pleading note she could hear in his voice? Hardly, she acknowledged, tensing her body against the longing invading her.

'But not for much longer.'

She saw his face tighten, his eyes going hard and opaque. 'Have you told Alice?'

So he *hadn't* changed his mind. How on earth had she ever thought he might?

'Did you expect me to? I'd better go in. It's Anna's day off, and I'm going to prepare dinner. Oh——' she turned and looked at him '——while you've been away, I've . . . I've moved back into my old room. I . . . I thought it was best.'

She had told Anna and Alice that the double bed in Luke's room hurt her back, and that she preferred the single bed in the guest room she had previously occupied. And, because she was pregnant, both of them had accepted her excuse at face value.

She had expected Luke to be relieved, but instead he was looking at her almost as though he hated her. Perhaps he *did* hate her, she thought dully. Perhaps he hated her because every time he looked at her he must wish she was Louise. And when he knew she was carrying his child, it would be even worse.

She almost ran into the house, not bothering to look and see if Luke was following her.

It was true that she had to prepare the evening meal, but most of the work was already done.

She had burned slightly outside in the hot sun, and her skin felt tight and hot. She was also very tired and irritable, she admitted as she changed for dinner.

Alice was having her meals in the dining-room now, instead of on a tray in her room. She was coming out of her room just as Sara went downstairs.

'What a lovely surprise for you, Sara,' she exclaimed. 'Having Luke home early. I expect he was worried about you...'

Worried that she might try and hold him to their marriage, possibly, Sara thought bitterly.

She was glad of Alice and Tom's company over dinner. Without it, it would have been a nightmare.

Luke barely spoke to her, and every mouthful of food she ate felt as though it would choke her.

'I'm going swimming with Ian tomorrow,' Tom announced for Luke's benefit halfway through the meal. 'His dad came round to see us, didn't he, Sara?'

'Yes.' She said it briefly. After all, Alan Jessop's visit was hardly of importance to her. He had come round solely to thank her again for taking care of Ian, and they had spent a little more than five minutes together. He had been on his way to Chester at the time, and had also issued the invitation to Tom to join Ian and himself at a local leisure centre for an afternoon.

Sara wanted Tom to have friends of his own age, and so she had agreed, but now Luke was looking at her with a thunderous expression that made Alice chuckle.

'Oh, dear, now I'm afraid you've made Luke jealous, darling! You needn't worry, Luke,' she teased. 'Poor Sara hasn't been well enough to do anything to make even the most possessive husband jealous. This pregnancy...'

Horrified, Sara stood up, clattering plates and talking desperately, looking everywhere but at Luke. She rushed out to the kitchen, shaking violently as she put down the dirty plates. Oh, God, of all the ways for him to find out!

She heard the door open behind her and knew that it was him.

'Is this true?' he demanded quietly.

'What?' She tried to make her voice light and disinterested. 'That I haven't done anything to make you jealous?'

'Sara...' The ominous warning in his voice silenced her. 'Are you carrying my child?'

'I am carrying *a* child,' she told him quietly, keeping her back to him.

'*My* child?' He took hold of her and swung her round so that he could look into her eyes. '*My child...*'

This was getting out of hand. She had to do something, and fast.

'Luke, I know you don't want this. It won't make any difference to our divorce, I promise you.'

'Oh, my God!'

She ignored his muttered curse and went on doggedly, 'I *know* when you married me it was to punish me... I *know* how much you loved your first wife... I *know* my child can never...'

A horrid shaft of weakness struck her, and she clutched at the worktop with a small moan. She was going to faint. She shouldn't have rushed up from the table like that.

In the distance she heard Luke curse, his voice hoarse and strained, and then he was picking her up and it felt so lovely to be in his arms again that she gave a soft sigh and curled trustingly against him.

When she came round, she was lying on a bed. No, on *Luke's* bed, she realised, struggling to sit up, and finding she couldn't because of the hard arm imprisoning her.

'Sara, we have to talk.'

'About the divorce?' She couldn't look at him.

'No,' Luke told her slowly, 'about my first marriage. You never knew Louise. She was nothing like you, not in looks nor in personality. I met her in Melbourne. She was a city girl through and through. She did part-time modelling.'

Sara could picture her, a slim, willowy, blonde beauty with the sophistication and poise she herself could never have.

'We dated several times. We made love.' He shrugged. 'She was a very beautiful woman, and I was only human. And then I didn't see her for some time. I was away on business. When I came back, she got in touch with me. She told me she was pregnant and the child was mine.'

He wasn't looking at her, but Sara could feel the tension building inside him.

'You're a very sensitive woman, and I think you can possibly understand what it meant to me—a man who'd lost his parents at a very young age and then been passed from one set of foster parents to another, to know he'd fathered a child. We were married a week later.' He caught her face in his hands, and tilted it so that he could look into her eyes.

'I didn't love Louise and she didn't love me, but I thought that didn't matter. I thought my responsibility for the child I had fathered was more important than our mutual lack of love.

'And then Louise was offered a big modelling contract. She was waiting for me one night when I came home from a trip up country. She told me she was accepting the contract and that she'd had a termination. "Got rid of it," that was how she put it, while I'd been out of the city on business. I wanted to kill her.'

He said it emotionlessly, but Sara could see the way his hands opened and closed, and her stomach tightened unbearably. What he was telling her had no bearing at all on the life she had thought he and her cousin had lived, none at all.

'I told her she had no right to get rid of my child.' He grimaced suddenly, a tired, defeated man, Sara recognised. 'That was when she told me that the child wasn't even mine, but that its father was a photographer she had known for some time. Another free spirit like herself.

'We had the most God-almighty row. She left... I discovered later that she'd gone back to her parents. She was killed three days after in a car accident with her father. At the time, I thought it was divine justice. I felt no pity for her... no regrets. I was like a man turned to stone, and I've remained like a man turned to stone ever since. At least until... Oh, God, Sara,' he begged harshly. 'Don't leave me! I need you too much. I need you... I need our child. Stay with me.'

She started to trembled violently. 'But you don't love me.'

He laughed savagely. 'Oh, no? I loved you from the moment I saw you,' he told her fiercely. 'I loved you and I hated myself for it. I wanted to tear that love out of my heart and destroy it . . . I told myself there was no way I was going to let myself love any woman, but especially a woman like you—cold-hearted, greedy, unfeeling.

'And yet, with everything you did, everything you said, everything you are, you confounded me . . .'

'You married me to punish me!'

'And ended up punishing myself,' he groaned. 'I might have said I married you to punish you. I might even have believed it myself, but I didn't make love to you to punish you. I made love to you because I couldn't stop myself. Because I had to have the sweetness of you.' He took a deep, steadying breath, and withdrew from her slightly. 'I tried to do the right thing—to set you free by divorcing you—but I can't—not now.

'If a divorce is what you want, somehow I'll have to resign myself to letting you go. I can't hold you a prisoner to my love.'

Her mouth started to quiver, and he lifted his hand and gently probed her bottom lip with his thumb. A shaft of pure sensation convulsed her, her eyes going wild with hunger and hope.

'Oh, God, don't look at me like that.'

'Like what?'

'Like you want me to take you in my arms and do this,' he responded indistinctly, his arms closing round her, his mouth probing urgently at the trembling softness of her lips, parting them so that he could savour her sweetness.

She clung blindly to him, welcoming the fierce heat of his kiss, the powerful force of his heartbeat, the heat and strength of him. The kiss lasted a long time. Long enough to make her head spin and her body go taut with desire.

'Now say it,' he demanded huskily as he released her.

'Say what?'

'That you'll stay with me . . . You *can't* respond to me the way you do and not feel something,' he groaned. 'Not my sweet Sara, you're too honest . . . too . . . too womanly to respond to a man in that way without feeling something for him.'

'I love you,' Sara admitted huskily. 'And there's nothing more I want from life than to be your wife and bear your child—your children,' she amended, laughing slightly in protest at the fierceness of his embrace.

'Our child.' He touched her stomach possessively. 'It will be a girl, of course. Alice would be furious if it wasn't. Tom will spoil her to death, and so will I . . .'

'Are you sure it's me you love?' Sara dared to tease from the security of her new-found love. 'Or is it just this?'

She patted her stomach and looked at him.

'It's you,' Luke told her soberly. 'I can't deny that I love knowing that you've conceived my child, Sara, but if there was no child, if there was never to be a child, it would still be you.'

For the first time, she was the one to kiss him—
holding his face in the cup of her hand while she
tenderly drew her lips against the hardness of his,
and gloried in the fierceness of his response to her.

'Fitton? What sort of a name is that?' Tom demanded staring down at the tiny pink and white
occupant of the crib.

'Exactly the right sort of name for my very first
great-granddaughter,' Alice told him firmly.

They had crept into the nursery together to
admire its new occupant. Sara had only been home
from hospital a matter of hours. She was downstairs with Luke.

'They're in his study, kissing,' Tom had reported
to Alice in disgust, and without a word being said
both of them had made their way up here to survey
their new relative.

'Fitton,' Tom said the name again experimentally, and then announced with masculine superi-
ority, 'Well, I suppose it's all right for a girl.'

Fitton opened her blue eyes and stared solemnly
at him, and then, having approved of what she saw,
she yawned and went straight back to sleep.

Downstairs in the study, Luke released Sara reluctantly. 'You don't know how much I've missed
you . . .'

'Luke, I've only been gone three days,' she reminded him softly, and then added, 'I've missed
you, too.'

Luke groaned as he took her back in his arms, kissing her gently.

'Some day soon, I'm going to let you show me just how much.'

And, some day soon, she did.

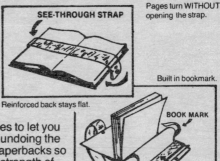